THE SPIDER:
GREEN GLOBES OF DEATH

MASTER OF MEN!

SPIDER®

GREEN GLOBES
OF DEATH

By Grant Stockbridge

STEEGER BOOKS • 2020

PUBLISHING HISTORY

"Green Globes of Death" originally appeared in the March 1936 (Vol. 8, No. 2) issue of
The Spider magazine. Copyright 2020 by Argosy Communications, Inc. All rights
reserved.

CHAPTER 1
DANSE MACABRE

WENTWORTH WATCHED the girl in scarlet saunter toward him and, when she glided to a halt, he swept her a bow that made his black cape swirl... but he did not lose sight of the two men in costume who watched him with hostile furtiveness from across the ballroom. A masquerade dance might not seem a place for murder, but Wentworth thought that he could read the will to kill in those two men—to kill Wentworth, who had worn to the masquerade the costume of—the Spider! The girl's blue eyes were intent from behind a silken mask....

"Does the Spider dance?" she asked mockingly, half-lifting her warm bare arms in invitation. A black patch beside her faintly smiling mouth was shaped like a heart.

Wentworth laughed lightly. He could appreciate beauty, even when it came to him in treachery as this girl undoubtedly did. There was another reason for laughter: he had come tonight in the costume of the Spider as a deliberate challenge to a new and rising criminal power, and, beyond question, this charming girl in scarlet and powdered wig brought him the enemy's answer!

"The Spider dances, yes," he told her gravely, "but not to measures that you would enjoy. I understand there are benches in the conservatory...." He offered his arm, letting his thin, hard lips curve upward. It was not a pleasant thing, that smile,

1

but Wentworth knew there were reasons other than his facial expression for the faint shudder which abruptly shook the girl's slim shoulders. The girl might not know that he was actually the Spider; but even a man disguised as the Spider became a sinister and ominous creature. Throughout the world, he was known as a merciless avenger. More than a hundred criminals had died with the mocking red seal of the Spider upon their foreheads— and some had died horribly.... Small wonder then, that the girl

The lobby was strewn with bodies of men and women in gala evening attire!

shuddered when the Spider offered his arm! She covered her fright with a trilling laugh, put a white hand almost caressingly upon his arm….

"Is it… *safe* to have a rendezvous with the Spider?" she whispered.

"Treachery is never safe," Wentworth informed her flatly, and his eyes went deliberately to the two men who kept watch—

one costumed as a cavalier with his palm upon the pommel of a long sword, the other in fool's motley, his bell stick like a battle mace. They were moving deftly across the crowded dance floor toward the darkened conservatory to which Wentworth was leading the girl….

"*Treachery?*" the girl gasped.

Wentworth bowed his head. His eyes were mocking. "I am certain that the escort of such a charming lady as you will consider your desertion… *treachery!*"

THE GIRL'S answering laughter, as they entered the conservatory was off-key. That of the Spider was strangely flat and mocking, a challenge to whomsoever might be lurking in the shadows. Enemies were behind him and at his side. There well might be others in hiding…. He felt his blood quicken. He had come ready to fight. How else could the Spider enter the home of Charles Holland, whose brother the Spider had killed?

Wentworth had not been invited to the masquerade—men do not soon forget the slaying of their brothers, even though that brother had been a criminal—but it had seemed the best way to attack the new uprising of the Underworld which Wentworth feared. His life was dedicated to the defense of the people against the wolves of injustice, and it seemed that the shrewdest foe he had ever fought was come to life again!

When Jack Holland, brother of Wentworth's involuntary host, had turned criminal, he had taken for himself the name of the Fly, as a deliberate taunt to the Spider. His genius for successful slaughter and robbery had united the entire Underworld behind the leadership of his gold-hilted knife—which was crested, mockingly, with the image of a fly.

Almost he had smashed the powers of law and order; almost he had defeated and slain the Spider. In the end, Wentworth had triumphed. But now, amazingly, the Fly had struck again!

Openly, and with the unrivaled daring which only the Fly had ever shown before, this new Fly had murdered the Mayor of New York City! And he had left his fly-crested knife buried in the Mayor's heart as a token and a challenge!

Suspicion of Jack Holland's younger brother, Charles, had seemed ridiculously obvious, yet it was a line of investigation Wentworth could not ignore. He had chosen the direct, frontal attack of crashing Charles Holland's masquerade in the costume of the Spider. His host, seeing him as he entered, had stiffened, his frosty blue eyes going cold. But he had not challenged… until now. In the twilight of the conservatory, Wentworth seated the girl upon a marble bench, stood before her with both hands upon the head of his cane.

"I'm afraid," he said gently, "that we will shortly be interrupted. Won't you first unmask?"

Through the easy banter of his voice, his ears were acutely attuned. It was one of the Spider's favorite tricks, to be on guard while seeming totally unaware of approaching danger. He twisted the head of his cane slightly to the left. He did not grip it in his fist, but held it across his palm between thumb and fingers as a man grasps the hilt of a sword…. There could be no doubt that Holland, or certainly some of his guests, had understood the nature of his challenge, knew that no one without the right would dare to wear the costume of the Spider.

The girl sat with a rigidity that betrayed her tension, her hands folded in her lap upon the looped and flounced silk of her period gown. Her elaborate, powdered coiffure seemed too heavy for the slender column of her throat and Wentworth read fright in her eyes. She was new to this game of treachery and death…. She came abruptly to her feet, took a step forward, hands reaching out.

"Leave here before it is too late," she said quickly. "Please, don't wait for explanations. I… *Oh!*"

IF THIS was new treachery, it was cleverly executed. Her voice, the fervor of her pleading face, would have prevented any man less alert than Wentworth from hearing the approach of his enemies. As it was, he had to thrust her sharply away lest she interfere with his defense. The girl fell, rather than sat, upon the bench and Wentworth spun about with a litheness which his assumed limp and hunched shoulders would seem to make impossible. He was instantly on guard, the cane in his right hand with its ferrule forward and just touching the floor. The two men who had watched him were within three paces of the Spider! The cavalier's sword was a gleam of deadly steel in his right hand and the man in motley gripped his bell stick like a club. Through the holes in their masks, their eyes were glittering beads.

"Leave us, Lou," the cavalier ordered the girl, and with the words, Wentworth recognized him. He had changed his evening dress, which he had worn in the reception line, for the silks of a period costume, but the voice was unmistakable. It was Charles

6

Holland. The girl got to her feet and moved toward him…. He thrust out his left hand in a stiff gesture.

"Leave us, Lou," he repeated.

Lou hesitated, her head swinging as she looked first at Holland, then at Wentworth. Her slim shoulders slumped and she stumbled toward the door that gave on the gaiety of the ballroom.

"Close the doors, Shock, and guard them," Holland said then, and the man in motley backed away. The closing of the doors turned the orchestra and the laugher into a faint, distant music. Holland lifted his sword in salute. "You have a sword in your cane," he said bitterly to Wentworth. "You have challenged me, and I would not decline if I could."

Wentworth laughed sharply. He flicked his wrist and the wooden sheath slithered musically from his cane sword, left the steel glittering in his hand.

"Why did you kill the Mayor, Holland?" he asked. "And especially, why have you taken your brother's *nom de crime?*"

Holland replied raspingly, "On guard, Spider!" His rapier sang against Wentworth's steel. "I'm going to kill you!"

Wentworth's thinned lips smiled slightly. He feinted for the left breast, tapped Holland's blade hard, circled—and lunged like lightning for the right breast. But his adversary's parry was swift and sure, and a *riposte* missed Wentworth's throat only because his recovery was of a speed that had never been surpassed on the mat of any *salle d'armes* of the world. Wentworth smiled and nodded. Holland's dead brother had been superb with the saber. Holland was master of the rapier. This would be no easy task....

The blades rang harshly as Holland began a fiery attack. Wentworth stood firm, steely wrist turning thrust and lunge in bewildering sequence. He perceived abruptly what Holland was trying to do. Behind Wentworth was a narrow passageway between high waving fronds of palm and fern. There might be other men hidden there! If Holland could only drive him back into that corridor.... A lunge so swift and savage that it was impossible to turn forced Wentworth to leap backward a full yard. His *riposte* kept Holland from pressing the advantage, but Wentworth was dangerously close to the shrubs.

THERE WAS a smile on Holland's lips to match Wentworth's own. Even when death hovered over their heads, these two could joy in the fight for its own sake. Their swords glinted in the twilight of the conservatory, found each other as much by instinct as by vision. Each thrust found its parry; every *riposte* was warded. Wentworth's right forearm had been scratched, Holland had felt the sting of the point upon his cheek. He could not force Wentworth back another foot, but neither could Wentworth fight his way out into clear floor space again. And there was always the consciousness that there might be more men hidden there behind the flowers.

It was the Spider who broke the deadlock. He had never been a conventional swordsman. He knew the French and Italian schools of fence, the tricks of a score of masters. It was apparent that Holland was equally familiar with the rapier. It was obvious to Wentworth that, if he were to triumph, he must go outside all he had learned, ignore precedent and danger…. Without a preliminary flourish, he broke the half-instinc-

tive rhythm of thrust and parry, lunge and *riposte*. He did a thing many expert swordsmen would have feared to attempt because of its overwhelming peril. An inch of miscalculation, a moment's misreading of his opponent's intentions…!

He sensed that Holland planned a lunge, the most savage and violent attack which can be made with the rapier. Even as the thought flicked through Wentworth's mind, Holland struck. His arm shot out and behind the leveled blade, he hurled the entire weight of his body. He bounded clear of the floor, left leg trailing behind him for balance, right knee cushioned upward against his body to catch his weight and hurl him backward on guard should his attack fail. But he did not intend to fail. All the pent-up hatred of the years that had passed since his brother's death went into it. And Wentworth did not attempt a parry!

He should have caught the tip of his opponent's sword close against the hilt of his own, turned it aside and attempted to *riposte* with a swift thrust before Holland could recover. He knew that *riposte* was impossible. However swiftly he thrust after a parry, he was too slow to catch Holland before the man returned to his original position, blade on guard.

Wentworth shut his lips grimly and threw his life into the

balance. If he miscalculated by an inch, he would be run entirely through by that fiercely darting sword, but he took that chance as he had taken a thousand before. Instead of parrying, he swayed his body aside at the hips and his rapier licked out for the breast of Charles Holland!

The maneuver was perfectly executed. Holland's point ripped through Wentworth's coat, but missed flesh. Wentworth's sword pierced—and then Wentworth did a queer thing—a mad thing! Instead of driving his point home with stiffened arm and shoulder, he threw his hand up, as if he had driven a harmless foil button against an opponent's plastron in a friendly assault!

HOLLAND'S GRIN had twisted into a surprised grimace in that last instant. He had failed, had felt the point of the man he strove to kill prick the skin above his heart—and he still lived! Holland recovered from his lunge, faltered backward and dropped the point of his sword. His left hand went slowly to his breast, where Wentworth's sword had pricked and the warmth of his own blood wet his fingers. He knew it was no serious wound. His eyes met Wentworth's....

"Why?" he whispered. "You could have killed me, yet you spared my life. Why?"

Wentworth himself was frowning. He had come here this night for the express purpose of determining whether Charles Holland was the Fly, and killing him if he were guilty. Holland had attacked him, had not denied the charges and yet, when the moment came to strike, the Spider's hand, which never before had faltered, had swerved from its task!

"Why?" Holland repeated.

Wentworth shook his head and the man in motley sprang from the shadows to Holland's side. "Master Charles!" he cried. "In the ballroom. Robbers! *The Fly!*"

Holland and Wentworth both whirled toward the man costumed so garishly in the green and red dress of a fool. A bell on his cap jingled softly as he nodded.

"The Fly," he cried urgently, "is robbing your guests, Master Charles!"

CHAPTER 2
MASQUE OF DEATH

WENTWORTH WAS instantly in motion, charging toward the doors with long, smooth bounds, his black cape whipping backward from his shoulders. He thrust the puzzle of his failure to kill Charles Holland completely out of his brain. That was something which leisure must resolve, and here was a problem that demanded immediate cyphering. In the ball room, the Fly, who had been his enemy through one of the gravest battles of his career, was robbing the wealthy guests of Charles Holland!

He was wrong in one thing, Wentworth corrected himself as he ran. This could not be the same Fly whom he had fought previously. He and that first Fly had dueled with swords on a narrow bridge a half dozen stories above the street. In the end, the Spider's saber had slipped through and the Fly had fallen nearly a hundred feet to the pavement below.... No, this must be some other killer trading in on the Fly's prestige....

11

Just outside the closed doors of the ball room, Wentworth checked his plunge and found that Charles Holland was close beside him, rapier still in hand. Together, these two who had sought to kill each other, peered through the curtained glass. A muffled oath squeezed out through Holland's teeth and he ripped open the door, darted through. Wentworth reached out to snatch him back and a savage blow from behind drove him to his knees. First numbness, then pain lanced across Wentworth's shoulder, through his nape, and his sword cane skittered across the polished floor. He braced his body on stiffened arms, was dimly aware that Holland, sword lifted high above his head, was rushing forward.

"After me, Shock!" he cried and his voice reached Wentworth as from a great distance.

Something struck the floor beside the Spider with savage violence and he realized that it had been the man Shock who slugged him and that a second blow had been averted only by Holland's shout.... The ball room was in tableau before the dazed Spider. Along one wall stood all the women, hands raised, their pale faces at stark contrast with their gay costumes, facing them stood the men—two bandits with sub-machine guns, whose muzzles roved with ceaseless hunger, held them motionless. A third robber, seeming no more than a boy in a gay scarlet raiment of a court page, was gathering the jewels and money surrendered by the prisoners. And ranged before the leader who stood, weaponless, to supervise the work, were Charles Holland with his challenging sword and the man in motley who served him.

Wentworth was aware of all these things without conscious inspection, for his eyes went inevitably to the leader, to the Fly! He stood between the two machine gunners at the end of the long hall and the mere sight of him jerked Wentworth to his feet as if—his nerves had been shocked by galvanic batteries. He could not mistake that dapper, smiling man with the lazy, savage eyes of black and the suavely cruel face. It was... *the Fly!*

ONCE MORE Wentworth scoffed at himself, at his involuntary mental recognition of this man as the one he had slain. The Spider's piercing eyes narrowed to the inspection. He reminded himself deliberately that the entire identity of that other Fly had been assumed—that the, face, even the color of the eyes had been a manufactured thing. There was no reason why another crook could not do as Holland's dead brother had, build the face of the fly over his own. No, no, the Fly was dead, and this man... a mere impostor.

Wentworth's brain, with the facility of long training, had snapped back to normal. He knew that the man called Shock had struck him with the bell stick and he did not understand why; nor did he understand why Charles Holland, alone before that deadly killer and his machine gunners, had been allowed to approach unscathed; unless... unless he and the Fly were allies!

Wentworth's gaze returned to the Fly. The killer was garbed from head to foot in a monk's black robe. The hood was dropped back from his smooth blond head and, at the waist instead of a rope girdle, he wore twin gun holsters from whose open tops thrust the butts of heavy revolvers. So far, no one had been injured among the guests, but Wentworth remembered the

Fly's work of old. Always, the killer had covered his tracks with a brutal massacre!

The Fly bowed to Wentworth. "An unexpected pleasure," he murmured. He turned to a machine gunner. "Wilson, give the gentleman in black your entire attention. If he so much as blinks an eyelid, empty your entire drum of bullets into his carcass. He is the Spider!"

The man called Wilson turned a paling face and a menacing gun muzzle upon Wentworth. His eyes burned. He crouched in his eagerness. Wentworth smiled slightly. That order was very typical of the Fly's alertness, but he would have been much wiser had he ordered the man to shoot immediately.

Charles Holland was speaking angrily....

"I demand that you leave this house immediately," he cried. "You are an impostor, attempting—to dishonor my brother's memory. He has made his atonement and..." Holland took a short, furious step forward, his rapier coming up. The Fly did not move, but his hands, hanging loosely at his sides, were very close to his revolvers. The men were ten feet apart. A fierce lunge....

The Fly said drily, "Don't try it, my dear brother, though I appreciate your defense of my name. I'd hate to soil my hands with fratricidal blood...."

Holland reeled and a hoarse cry pushed from his throat. The Fly smiled slightly, looked beyond him at the boy who was collecting jewels. "Hurry there, Gary. We haven't much time...."

Wentworth pulled his eyes from the stricken horror on Charles Holland's face and looked toward the boy who was collecting the loot. A woman had echoed the name uttered by

The rapier struck and the gun fell from the Fly's right hand!

the Fly, and her voice was a gasp. "Gary, *Gary....!*" It was the girl in scarlet, the one who had led him into Holland's trap. Her hands were reaching out in appeal to the man in page's scarlet. She started from the line of women, and the machine gunner on guard rasped a curse and jerked the snout of his weapon toward her. She ignored that, caught the man she called Gary by the arm.

"You can't do this, Gary," she cried. "In heaven's name, what are you doing here with that... that *beast!*"

GARY LOOKED shamed. He peered over his shoulder toward the Fly, who was smiling, though not pleasantly. "Well, Gary," he drawled. "The lady is charming, but we have no time now for dalliance...."

Gary jerked his arm from the girl's hand, slapped her heavily across the face with the back of his hand and sent her reeling against the wall. "Tend to your own business," he said roughly. The girl—Wentworth remembered her name was Lou—sagged against the wall, her eyes large and frightened above the hand she pressed to her cheek. Holland shouted out hoarsely and took a quick stride toward Gary, but a drawled word from the Fly stopped him. The machine gunners were jittery. It would take very little to make them release their thunderous death....

Wentworth watched the whole scene with hard, narrowed eyes. He did not quite understand what had happened there. He did not think that Gary was the girl's lover. Holland might more accurately be thought to hold that position. But it was all of a piece with the usual cruelty of the Fly. It was not unlikely that the Fly had planned just this scene, knowing of a relationship between his minion and a guest at Holland's masquerade.... Swift anger, and doubt, raced over Wentworth. Already in his own mind, he was classing this killer before him with that other Fly whom he had fought—and slain, he swore—months ago. He claimed to be the same man.... But all that did not matter. What was of importance was the man's assertion that he was the Fly, for it undoubtedly portended another such crime as those which had shocked a world when the Fly was in his heyday. It meant that he would conclude this polite looting with slaughter!

Wentworth's hands ached for his guns. Somehow, and it must be quickly! The Spider must evade the menace of that machine gun and kill the Fly. He was certain that the Fly did not mean that the Spider should survive this night. He was delaying assassination only because he did not wish shots to give the alarm before he had completed his work....

Wentworth, after the first look, had not glanced again toward the machine gunner. The man's attention was much more apt to wander if the Spider did not hold his eyes.... If only some one would create a diversion, the Spider could go into action.

It would be the work of much less than a second to bring his guns into play. But he could not count on help. The girl's cry had caused a few moment's disturbance, but she was quiet now, standing with her head very high, not even looking at the boy who was collecting the loot. There were both pride and fear on her face....

Wentworth smiled in the direction of the Fly and began to whistle softly between his teeth. The tune was piercing and dwelt on minor notes, such as he used sometimes to summon his

Hindu servant, Ram Singh. The doughty Sikh was not within call tonight, but the Fly, who knew the Spider's habits so well, would not know that.… The Fly whipped about savagely.

"Quiet!" he shouted. "Wilson, he's trying to call that Hindu servant of his. You'd better go to the door and then take a gander through the conservatory. I'll watch Mr. Spider." He drew the revolvers with a movement as swift and smooth as thought. "If you make a sound.…"

Wentworth shrugged at the guns, his lips derisive. "Sorry, I was merely whistling away a dull moment." There were only three bandits left to fight against now.…

The Fly's heavy black gaze was upon Wentworth. His face took on sharp, venomous lines. Disguised his countenance undoubtedly was, but it was suited admirably to his character. It was plain that he wavered between greed for more jewels and the mad urge to murder. Delay would bring more wealth into his pouch, but it exposed him for long minutes to this calm, black-robed killer. However calm and self-confident a criminal might be, he could not gaze with equanimity on the Spider. Too many such men as he had died by that deadly hand—had been found by police with that mocking red seal shaped like a Spider on their foreheads.… The Fly's right gun came up slowly to sight on the Spider's breast. The Fly's mouth twitched. He had

18

to choose between caution and greed and his fear of the Spider was conquering. He would kill him now!

THE THING happened then for which Wentworth had been playing. He had seen concentrated hostility upon the face of Charles Holland, standing stiff and straight with his rapier in his hand. If only he could pull the Fly's attention wholly away from Holland for a brief moment, even at the cost of risking a shot at himself....

Even as the Fly leveled the revolver, Holland struck with the speed that Wentworth had found so nearly fatal—a long, straight lunge in which sword and body united into a single, striking weapon. The rapier struck, and the gun fell from the Fly's right hand, blasting futilely into the floor.

Furiously, the Fly whipped his second revolver about. But Holland followed his lunge with a leap forward that brought him breast to breast with the man who had called him brother....

Wentworth cursed raggedly. The instant Holland struck, his hands whipped beneath his cloak to the twin automatics that nestled beneath his arms. He crouched now with them ready in his fists—and they availed him nothing! He had seen that Holland, instead of wounding the Fly, had clicked his rapier point against the revolver itself and hurled it from the Fly's hand. That was understandable, since nothing except a blow against the weapon would have saved Wentworth. What had happened afterward was more strange. Holland had made no attempt to injure the Fly with his sword! Surely, he did not believe that claim of brotherhood! Yet, it must be so. For, breast to breast, he wrestled with the Fly and his body was a perfect shield against the Spider's lead.

Wentworth sprang across the floor with long, bounding strides, seeking a position from which to strike, and... *the room exploded!*

A concussion soundless as a vacuum burst upon the crowd. The ceiling chandeliers swung in crazy circles and crashed; a wall dissolved in a blast of red fire and the floor rose up under Wentworth's feet and struck him on the chest. He scrambled to his feet, peering through the momentary blackness.

The fall had destroyed his sense of direction. He groped for the spot where the Fly and Holland struggled, and, in the thick darkness, a shot crashed out and women screamed on a wild, tearing note.

The darkness vanished in a flickering red dance of flame which pushed up through the floor and in from three walls of the room. Outside in the night, a machine gun cackled into deadly action and, even above the cries of panic-stricken women and the mounting turmoil of the flames, Wentworth could hear the nearby thud of bullets. He could tell, too, when they found flesh from the frenzied cries which were wrung from the stricken.

Wentworth stood stock-still and tried to orient himself. His face was twisted in fierce anger. The Fly was playing his old tricks again, covering his tracks with slaughter—turning loose fire and murder in a holocaust which would blot out all thought of pursuit. The fumes of burning gasoline were stifling. Somewhere, the Fly was racing to safety with his killers, and the Spider....

With a groan, Wentworth recognized the keenness of the

Fly's strategy. Even the Spider could not abandon these poor helpless souls to the death the Fly had planned for them, though it meant that the murderer would escape. The Fly's plan would succeed now, but there would be a reckoning when the Fly paid for each second's misery of this night. *The Spider swore it!*

Throwing a quick glance about him, Wentworth spotted the doors of the conservatory through the thick lurid glare of the flames. "This way!" he shouted, making for the doors. "This way to safety!" He stumbled over a crumpled body, heaved the woman's limp form to his shoulder. *"This way to safety...!"*

CHAPTER 3
THE FLY HUNTS THE SPIDER!

WENTWORTH BEGAN the rescue work in a tearing rage. Everything in him cried out for the necessity of rescuing these people, trapped by walls of fire, but it was damnable to be so close to the Fly and then to fail.... Through the conservatory, with the woman's limp body across his shoulder, Wentworth raced. There were windows on the far side and he caught up a light bench and hurled it through the glass. The breakage made a draft, would suck the flames to fury, but there must be an exit and those gasoline-born flames had blocked all others.

Beside the broken window he whirled about, found a man reeling toward him. "Get out through that window," he ordered. "Carry this woman to a safe place and come back. There will be more."

The man looked at him without reason and Wentworth's right palm flicked hard and flat against his cheek. Anger flared briefly in the man's eyes, then came recognition and fear. He shrank back and when Wentworth repeated the order, he obeyed. The Spider raced back to the ballroom…. There was plenty of light cast by lurid flame. But fumes and black roiling smoke made the scene hazy. Men stumbled blindly about, racked by coughing, blinded by heat and vapor. Some already had collapsed to the floor or else had fallen prey to the hammering of the machine gun which had signaled the explosion.

"This way!" Wentworth made his voice pierce the chaos of fire roar and whimpering tenor. "This way!" He attracted attention at last. A few turned toward him. He could make out Charles Holland, sword gone, carrying a woman in his arms. Another man whose face was not clear ran lithely among the trapped people, turning them toward the door where Wentworth shouted the way to safety. They got the ballroom cleared finally, though the last of the victims was snatched smoldering from the very teeth of the flames.

Wentworth stood in the smoke-filled conservatory and looked slowly about to make sure there were no more. He had counted eleven dead…. At his side, Holland panted and the other man who had helped stepped close and thrust out his hand.

"Heard a lot about you, Spider," he said hoarsely, "but I never expected to meet you. Glad now that I have. Name is Claiborne Lee. If you ever need help for this kind of work…."

Wentworth studied the man's sharply eager eyes and nodded.

He motioned the other two out of the window and would not leave until they had reached safety. He was afire with anger. Eleven dead and loot that would run into hundreds of thou-  sands—and the Fly had got clean away. There were fire department men working at last, and the police out there in the street would have thrown a cordon around the block....

Wentworth smiled bitterly as he drew into the shadows with the two men. Now that they could accomplish nothing, the police were here to make it hard for the Spider.... Holland turned toward him stiffly.

"I... I owe you an apology," he said awkwardly. "If it had not been for your help, many more of my friends might have died. And I... I tried to kill you. You had me at your mercy and did not run me through. I do not understand, Spider."

CLAIBORNE LEE broke in eagerly, his voice deep, and vibrant. "You mean, Holland, that the Spider bested you at rapiers? Gad, Spider, you must be quite a man. Holland is easily the city champion, and in France...."

"Shut up, Lee," Holland said roughly, "Spider, I want to apologize. I know that if... if you killed my brother, there was... just cause."

Wentworth bowed coldly. It was all very well for Holland to make pretty speeches, but he had spared the Fly when he might have driven his sword through the man's heart. That mercy had brought death to six women and five men there in the storm of flame and lead. He could not seriously believe that this Fly was his brother.... Wentworth's old suspicions of Holland returned sharply. It would not be the first time that a man had made a grandstand pretense of being himself a victim of the very criminal organization he directed...."

"If you will excuse me," Wentworth bowed. "There is a lady here I'd like to see...."

He stepped backward into the darkness of a clump of high shrubs. Claiborne Lee moved as if to stop him. Holland started a protest, but he was gone. Their eyes were dazzled by the high-licking flames that reached out heat into the chill March night and they did not see that the Spider had simply covered hands and face with his black cape and stepped behind a shrub. The two men moved off, hunting for him, and Wentworth left his place of concealment. He had spoken the truth. He wanted desperately to find Lou, the girl in scarlet whom he had allowed to lead him into the trap. He must make her talk. In the first place, she probably knew what part Holland played in the affairs of the Fly, and in the second, she had recognized the bandit who collected the stolen jewelry....

He spotted her presently, standing weakly beside an emergency station which an ambulance interne had hurriedly established. There was a listlessness about her entire body. The slope of her young shoulders was weary.... Wentworth circled through the shadows, for he dared not approach openly. Several times while he advanced he was forced to halt while men in uniform raced past, but finally he achieved a place in the darkness by a high hedge.

"Lou!" he called softly. He stepped into the edge of the light. "Lou, I want to talk with you!"

Lou stiffened, then whirled, her face eager. That faded as she glimpsed the caped figure in the half-light. She clung to the side of the ambulance, her face terrified. She glanced behind her as if seeking help.... Wentworth stepped forward and smiled into her eyes.

"I intend you no harm, Lou," he said softly. "Won't you come and talk with me a little while?"

The girl's panic did not lessen. Her blue eyes stared oddly at Wentworth, her lips parted. She was very lovely, with the red light of the fire playing upon the soft line of her warm, young shoulders....

"You didn't lead me into the trap," Wentworth told her. "I knew what was behind it and went willingly. I just wanted to ask you a few questions. Who are you? Who was the boy in red with the Fly? I'd like to help him. He can't be all bad."

SLOWLY, THE girl's fear faded. Men and women had always trusted Wentworth instinctively. It was as if the fine, generous character of the man pierced even through his disguise to touch her. "Oh, he *isn't* bad, Spider," she cried softly. "His companions are bad. He's my little brother, Spider. God help him, now he has...."

It was at that moment an automatic spoke from nearby. The girl screamed, driven forward to her knees by the impact of a bullet which Wentworth heard pluck into her soft flesh. Her hands clawed at Wentworth's arms as she pitched forward. He threw his arms about her, dragged her flat to the ground as a

Richard Wentworth

second shot crashed out. His lips were writhing in sudden rage. This poor child…. His automatic leaped to his hand. He rolled free of where Lou lay, without sound or motion, sought out the shrub from which those cowardly shots had sped. It was impossible to fire. Those shots had thrown the already terrified men and women into panic and their black silhouettes darted back and forth in front of and behind the shrub where the assassin had hidden….

Wentworth delayed only a moment to lay a gentle hand on the unconscious girl. She had been so fresh and eager....

His lips twisted into a harsh smile, Wentworth hurled himself back into the shadows, raced forward. So the Fly, too, had seen the danger of the girl! Woman killer!

Wentworth cursed raggedly as he darted toward the assassin. It came to him with overwhelming suddenness that this shooting was a further count against Charles Holland. Holland had known that Wentworth was hunting the girl and could easily guess the reason.... It was possible, of course, that the Fly had left a gunman behind to account for the girl, since she had identified one of his men....

The Spider's charge had not been a direct rush into the muzzle of the hidden gunman's weapon, but a circling movement which would bring him to the flank. It took time, but his eyes were

acutely watchful. He had detected no signs of a fugitive.... The spot was only a score of feet away now, on his right.

Wentworth crept forward, then rose slowly to his feet. It was quite apparent that no one was any longer behind the shrub. He saw that it would have been quite possible for the assassin to crawl away on hands and knees, keeping the shrub between the ambulance and himself.

Wentworth strode angrily to the spot, bent over to study the earth. There were knee-prints there, but the exploded shells were gone, giving sufficient proof of the man's coolness. Wentworth bent closer. The knee-prints retreated across the damp earth, reached the border of a patch of shrubbery and.... Wentworth barely choked back a cry of triumph! There in the mud was the print of a man's palm! Deftly, Wentworth scooped out the cake of earth and nested it in his hat.

SO INTENT had been Wentworth's pursuit that until now he had not noticed three policemen charging on the bush behind which the gunman had crouched, closing in on where the Spider now was hidden! The police would have no means of knowing that it had not been the Spider who had done the shooting. They would open fire on sight, and Wentworth would be helpless! For the Spider did not fight the police. He might violate laws, but though the police considered him a criminal, he was actually their staunchest ally. Against the men in blue, his deadly guns were quite useless....

Frowning, Wentworth faded back into the dense heart of the thicket. This would offer only brief sanctuary for the policemen would certainly beat through every inch of cover in their search for the assassin. Wentworth was further handicapped by the necessity of keeping that palm print of soft earth in its original condition. This palm-print would identify the killer as readily as his fingerprints, though police experts had not yet been able to devise a method of classification which would make palm-prints useful in criminal identification systems.

Wentworth threw a searching look through the night. His hiding place was on the skirts of the lurid firelight. Smoke and fumes whipped acridly downwind. The police were drawing dangerously close! Wentworth's thinned lips tightened. He had only the slimmest chance to escape, but he must avail himself of it, or be slain! With deft movements, he stripped off cape and draped it over a shrub, placed his hat atop it as if the Spider knelt in the darkness to give battle. The dirt with its precious print he folded carefully into a handkerchief and placed it in the heart of a shrub, among thick stems where no one could step…. The police were no more than fifty feet away, approaching cautiously behind ready guns. Wentworth crept toward them, deftly unloading an automatic as he went. From a pocket he drew a half dozen fresh cartridges whose noses were colored a bright red. He put one in the chamber of the automatic, held the others in his palm. The Spider was ready….

One of the policemen abruptly threw himself prone on the earth. "There he is!" he shouted. "There he is! *Surrender or we'll blast you to hell!*"

Wentworth muffled his mouth with his hands and laughed softly, the challenging mockery of the Spider. He wanted them to open fire, so that his own shots would not be conspicuous.

The other two policemen went prone, inching forward on elbows and toes, guns ready. The one who had first challenged pointed his revolver high and fired a shot....

"*Surrender!*" he cried again.

"Come and get me!" Wentworth challenged, still muffling his mouth. He held the muzzle of his automatic against his coat to conceal the powder flame and fired through it at the ground just ahead of the nearest policeman. The echo of his shot was drowned in a crashing fusillade that sent lead ripping through the shrubbery! The black cape of the Spider twitched to the pound of lead. Coolly, Wentworth worked the bolt of the automatic, ejecting the empty shell whose recoil had been too weak to throw it clear. He shoved another of the red-nosed cartridges into the gun, leveled it again.... Abruptly the policeman at whom he had first shot reeled to his feet with piercing cries, his hands clapped to his eyes. He danced in sharp agony....

"Tear gas!" he howled. "*Tear gas!*"

WENTWORTH SMILED in the darkness where he crouched and once more fired through the edge of his coat, thus hiding the flash. The cloth smoldered and he crushed it out between his palms, went about loading a third tear gas cartridge into the automatic. Before he was ready to fire again, the second policeman was rolling on the ground, coughing and groaning with the pain of the gas. In an hour or two, the men would be fully recovered, but for the moment the agony was intense. They could no more manipulate their guns than they could see. Wentworth fired his third shot, crept back to his cloak and hat. They must not be left behind to brand the Spider with the stigma of shooting that girl.... He drew his second automatic and sprayed singing lead high through the night, sending the men and women  who had been the restless spectators of the attack fleeing into the night.

Wentworth smiled pleasantly as he regained the dirt containing the palm print and, carrying cape and hat, stole away into the night. Matters had worked out much better than he had dared to hope. He still had to pass the police cordon, a line that would be drawn even tighter when word reached the line that a criminal was within. But for a man who could move with the silent ease of a shadow—to whose skilled touch any lock would yield—the task was not too difficult.... Wentworth scaled a fence, entered a house whose door lock he picked, climbed upward on ghostly feet to the roof, and traveled rapidly westward.

When he descended, outside the lines, the facial disguise of the Spider had vanished, and a taxicab sped him homeward. He would make a *moulage* cast of that palm print in the dirt and when he tracked down a suspect, he would carry in his pocket the proof of the man's guilt. There would be a special punishment for the man who had shot that gay young girl! By the Gods, the Fly should not again acquire a foothold in the Underworld, nor trod with murderous feet upon the necks of the people! The

Spider would find and kill him. Wentworth's modeled lips drew out thinly. His hand strayed to a gun....

A truck trundled out from a side street and dragged its length across the path of Wentworth's taxi. When the van filled the roadway from curb to curb, it stopped. Wentworth jerked erect in his seat. He whirled about and saw two autos spin around the corner and come racing toward him, saw that in each car men held weapons in their hands, sawed-off automatic shotguns and sub-machine guns. Even as he looked, they opened fire on him! Wentworth laughed sharply as he flung to his knees on the floor, guns leaping to his hands. The Spider might evade the police, but the Fly kept to his trail. If only the Fly had come to do his murder work in person....

CHAPTER 4
THE SPIDER IN A TRAP!

A S ALWAYS in emergency, Wentworth's mind leaped swiftly to the only possible defense—though even that would afford slim chance of escape. He ripped aside the glass panel that separated him from the driver of his taxi.

"Back up!" he shouted. "Back up full speed. *For your life!*"

As deftly as an old soldier finds cover, Wentworth had snatched at the narrow opening the attackers gave. Slamming in, with guns blasting death, they had made the mistake of separating to take the Spider from two sides at once. He was sure, abruptly, that the Fly was not present. He would not have left the way clear for the taxi to escape by a dash in reverse....

Now that Wentworth had pointed the way, the taxi driver saw what was needed and the gears snarled as he rasped into reverse and slapped his foot on the gas pedal. In the moment the cab started backward, a shot gun blasted twice from the car on the left and the driver slammed against his wheel, his hands beating against the air in a spasm of death. The back of his head….

Wentworth grated out a curse. The mockery that had lingered about his lips was wiped out and the glacial bleakness of his eyes, the thin harshness of his mouth were fearful things to see.

The cab continued backward, swerved slightly to the left, and the sway of the driver's limp body whipped the wheel in the opposite direction. The swerve was violent this time, and the cab slammed, back-first, into the attacking car on the right. Swaying, the killers' sedan skittered toward the curb, and Wentworth's taxi went into a slow, end-for-end spin.

The Spider was smiling again as he braced shoulders and knees against the seats. Brakes were shrieking as the killers tried to stop. A single sub-machine gun hammered at the spinning taxi, but all other weapons were silent. The Spider, an automatic pistol in either hand, took what shots the twisting cab allowed, and the unerring accuracy of years of practice sped his bullets true. He shot a back tire off the sedan the cab had rammed. He smashed a forty-five caliber slug through the brain of the machine gunner who had poked out the rear window of the other car. It took five shots to do these things, then the taxi hit the curbing broadside, teetered on two wheels and slapped over on its side on the walkway.

It was a new cab, its windows safety glass, and though they

33

shattered into myriad fragments, they did not rain Wentworth with dagger-like shards. He was wrenched from his braced position, thrown heavily on his shoulder against the roof of the cab. His hat fell from his head. The crisp, black locks of his hair straggled across his forehead and blood welled from a cut on his eyebrow. For one instant, flashing white lights danced before his eyes. He shook his head violently, got to his feet. He was standing on one door of the cab and its bottom with its steel frame and transmission formed a bulwark before him. It was not completely bullet-proof, but for the Spider it was enough…. He peered cautiously through a smashed window, guns ready.

THE SEDAN from which he had shot a tire was canted against the curb and three men were pouring from it. The second machine had stopped and one man, machine gun cradled against his hip, was crouched against its side. They were twenty yards away, Wentworth figured—just target range distance. His smile became an ugly twisted thing. His guns lifted calmly and fell on his targets….

History tells of famous marksmen who could make their sidearms do everything but speak Spanish, and modern tests have duplicated every feat that the records have revealed. There are at least three men in the United States who can duplicate the famous performance of Billy the Kid in which he shot two guns at once from the hip at dime-size targets thirty feet away and thirty feet from each other—and hit both! A matter of practice, of experience.

Richard Wentworth's life had depended on his automatics more times than he could remember. He had drilled with them

One wedged his shoulder into the door; another fired point-blank at Ram Singh!

until they were like nerve ends of his own brain. He fired four times and there were four dead men in the street. To be sure, their guns blasted at him, but their targets were only two moving guns and the upper half of a man's head. Their practice consisted of machine-gun work at ranges up to fifteen feet....

When he had fired the fourth shot, Wentworth stood motionless for a moment, seeing the last of his enemies squirm out his life in the street. His guns swung heavily to his sides, and he turned to the lifeless body of the taxi driver. Wentworth's keenly intelligent face was distraught. This man was innocent. He had died merely because it had been his misfortune to carry the Spider as a fare. His photograph grinned at Wentworth from his license card posted in the rear of the cab. Wentworth clamped his jaw shut hard. He drew out a notebook and scribbled down the man's name and address. At least, his people would not suffer want. That much the Spider could do....

Wentworth climbed out of the upmost door of the cab, tugged jerkily at the brim of his felt, shrugged his shoulders to settle the cape smoothly. He strode with hard, slapping heels toward the dead man.... It would have been impossible to tell which came first, the shot from the parked car, or Wentworth's flinching dodge which threw him three feet to the side and prone in the street; impossible except for one thing. Wentworth's right hand whipped a gun into view even before his body hit, and his weapon blasted in concert with the second shot from the cab. Then he climbed stiffly to his feet, brushed off his clothing. His lips moved in soundless curses. Childish of him to let that cab driver's death upset him so that he failed to realize that there must be at least one more man in that sedan. He had slain only two in that machine and gangster cars did not go forth to do murder with only two gunmen.

There was a set frown on his face as he slipped a platinum cigarette lighter from his vest pocket and stooped over each of the men he had slain. He pressed the base of the lighter to the foreheads of the dead, then he walked swiftly away.... The truck that blocked the street had long since gone, heads had popped out of a hundred windows and a police siren whimpered in the near distance. Two boys ran at Wentworth's heels, pointing fingers, shouting and capering. He disguised his manner of walking, kept his head tilted forward so that the broad brim of his black hat shaded his eyes. He had violated one of the few rules he had ever set for himself; he had used the seal of the Spider while in his own identity of Richard Wentworth! It meant his death on any one of a score of murder charges if police should be able to prove that the Spider and Wentworth were the same man. These boys and many of the people peering from their windows had seen him press his lighter to the foreheads of the dead, and when police arrived they would find gleaming there the blood-red *seal of the Spider!*

It had been necessary, Wentworth assured himself, even while he quickened his pace with the nearer approach of police sirens. The Fly had struck at him. It could not be allowed to pass without sending back the challenge, a dead man with the seal on his forehead....

WENTWORTH TURNED the corner not five seconds ahead of the first police car. He jumped into a taxi and the driver, who had been watching his approach, turned and ran. With an oath, Wentworth got behind the wheel and sent the cab racing up the street. He saw a man race to another taxi, saw it get under way.... The Spider had a lead of three blocks, and within minutes the entire radio patrol of the city would be on his trail, looking for him in the stolen taxi.... It took five minutes of swift maneuvering to make two turns out of sight of pursuit, then Wentworth abandoned the cab in the middle of the street at a red traffic light. Seconds later, he was lost in the early morning crowd that thronged the walks on the way to their various offices....

A half hour afterward, Richard Wentworth strolled into the foyer of the fifteen-story building that was his fortress against crime. He owned the entire structure, had bought it so that he could control the personnel and the tenancy. Here, if anywhere, the Spider could feel safe, but today he knew no sense of sanctuary. He was restless, harassed by thoughts of peril. The doorman bowed deferentially. A private elevator whisked him to his fifteen-room duplex penthouse and, within seconds of his entry, his white-haired old butler was relieving him of cape and hat. He looked down at them with a woodenness of expression on his ruddy face that Wentworth knew betokened his distaste. Not at the cut of the garments, for that was impeccable, but for the thing they represented, his master's constant duel with death....

Wentworth carefully handed Jenkyns the cake of hardening mud which contained a palm print. "Make a moulage cast," he told him, "and prepare me some prints from it. Be very careful. That print may hang a man...."

Jenkyns' old eyes followed his Master Dick lovingly as Wentworth strode briskly into his drawing room and threw  wide to the morning air the French doors that opened on the terrace. "Send Jackson to me," he called back.

Jenkyns' hand brushed the cape he carried with a slow, tender movement. He shook his head, started to turn away, then remembered....

"Miss Nita called, Master Dick," he said. A smile deepened the wrinkles of his mouth corners. That way lay Jenkyns' hopes. If only, now, Master Dick would marry....

Wentworth sucked in a deep breath of the brash spring air, closed the doors again and spun, clasping his lean, powerful hands together. He was a proud, arrogant man, built with a compact strength that was lithe and inconspicuous, but which gave him an appearance of solidity. The carriage of his shoulders and head was a banner of self-confidence, of quiet self-assurance too dignified for jauntiness. He smiled and nodded in answer to Jenkyns' message. "It's too early to disturb her just yet...."

"Oh, Master Dick," Jenkyns protested, "you know...." Then he realized that Wentworth was making a joke. Of course Miss Nita wasn't asleep, not while the master wore the garb of the Spider, not while he fought the Underworld. Jenkyns had shared some of those restless vigils which grew harder, rather than easier, as the months slid by.... He turned away to the telephone, his old head shaking gently. It was madness, but it was the sort of thing Master Dick would do. Afraid that, if he and the woman he loved, fulfilled their love in marriage and children, the grim hand of disgrace might touch them all....

HE REMEMBERED then to send Jackson to Wentworth and when he returned to the drawing room with the portable telephone, Jackson had left the building and Master Dick was in the music room, brushing the strings of his beloved Stradivarius to harmony. Wentworth was frowning, which was not his usual manner when he held his violin. The truth was that an increasing dread gripped him which even his music could not dispel.... He nodded to Jenkyns and the butler set the phone upon the concert grand beside which Wentworth stood, turned the transmitter toward him and went slowly from the room. Wentworth's lips curved tenderly. He nestled the violin under his chin, began to play....

It was one of his greatest delights, his violin. It gave him relief and rest when his soul and heart were torn as they had been this morning. Death and pillage lay ahead and the hand of the Spider would be mighty in vengeance—if he lived. But now let there be a little moment of peace while his heart sang to the woman he loved. Let the fingers which tomorrow, perhaps in an hour, might squeeze the triggers of his deadly guns, draw forth sweet music....

Afterward, Wentworth breakfasted, pheasant eggs whipped to a delicate froth in sherry that would have graced the table of a king, breasts of pigeons. Jenkyns had prepared them with his own hands. He had never been able to find a cook he thought worthy of his master. Then a shower, an alcohol rub and Wentworth forced his restless mind to sleep.

In a few hours he was up again. A second rub-down, fresh clothing when he arose for his luncheon with Nita, which she would share in his apartment, and he was as rested as if from hours on hours of sleep. Yet the feeling of relaxation and ease which usually attended this swift recuperative process failed to come to him. Even his Stradivarius could not beguile him and he strode restlessly from room to room while he waited for his Hindu body servant, Ram Singh, to bring Nita. He stalked back and forth upon his terrace. If he had not sent Jackson out on the Spider's business he could have a bout with the sabers. If it were true this Fly and that other were one, he would have need of all his skill….

Wentworth slammed the French doors behind him as he went indoors again, threw coat and cap carelessly to a chair. Impatiently, he jabbed a bell button and Jenkyns came on swift, silent feet.

"How long ago did Ram Singh leave to get Miss Nita?" he asked sharply.

Jenkyns took a heavy silver watch from his pocket and studied its face. "Just twenty minutes, Master Dick," he said gently. "In perhaps ten, minutes, sir…."

WENTWORTH HAD already stalked from the room. He knew what these moods of his portended. His nerves were crying aloud of danger. Not the peril that was a constant companion of his days and nights, but something imminent and heavy about him. Danger that would strike like a knife in the back…. He spun about, hand going to his lapel, to the guns that never left him, waking or asleep. Nothing, absolutely nothing here. He fled from the gymnasium to which he had wandered, loped again into the drawing room. There he halted himself, required of his muscles that they relax, that they keep him quiet for a full five minutes. Deliberately, he took out a cigarette and snapped flame to it from the same lighter that had a few hours before printed his signature of death upon the foreheads of six men.... He turned the lighter over curiously in his hand, looking at it with eyes that saw through and beyond it. How many times had that bit of gleaming metal touched the dead foreheads of his victims? A strong shudder shook him.

Wentworth was a gentle man by instinct. The arts held more appeal for him than for most other men. If he had not chosen the hard path of the Spider, he might have become the world's greatest virtuoso of the violin, a composer of note. Now and again, nature took this tool of the body and soul that he drove to such labors to exact the Spider's justice. Black despair....

Damn it, nothing could happen to Nita, not in the crowded streets of noon, not in his bullet-proof Daimler with that fierce Sikh, Ram Singh, at the wheel. He was a fool to worry, but his enemies had struck so many times at him through the woman he loved.... Abruptly, Wentworth snatched up his topcoat, belted it tightly about his waist, but left the lapels gaping wide. He stood for another minute staring before him toward the door that opened on the hall. He snatched a cap and strode out, walked restlessly about while he waited for the elevator, continued his pacing in the foyer on the first floor, his eyes straying ever and again to the curb before the marquis where presently Nita would alight…. Of course she would. He was mad to think… Ah, *there!*

The slim, chromium-slashed nose of the Daimler slid—into sight. The chauffeur stepped to the door to open it for Nita… and Wentworth hurled himself toward the street in a pounding sprint. Before he had slammed through the first set of doors, he had whipped out an automatic. He fired through the glass of the outer doors. The car that had pulled up just beside his own had poured out a flood of men, five of them with guns in their hands. They swept about the Daimler. The doorman went down beneath a hard-swung blackjack. Ram Singh attempted to slam shut the bullet-proof, self-locking doors and save Nita, but he was already too late. The Fly had prepared his men for that. One of them wedged his shoulder into the crack, leveled his gun at Nita. A second fired point-blank at Ram Singh….

CHAPTER 5
HOSTAGE TO DOOM

WENTWORTH'S FIRST shot, flung through the outer doors, caught the last man to leave the gang car and hurled him back against the driver. The—Spider was aware of muffled reports within the Daimler and knew that Nita's lighter automatic had gone into action, but there was no time even to look there. As he slammed out onto the pavement, he threw a second bullet at a gunman, just rounding the nose of the limousine to the attack. The lead spun him about and his hands clawed at the shining chromium as he went down. Wentworth swung toward the Daimler. Only one man was left on his feet and he was fleeing frantically toward the gang car. Even as Wentworth spotted him, he had put the bullet-proof bulk of the limousine before him as a shield....

Wentworth sprang to his car. With swift hands, he tugged aside the bodies of the two men who had fallen there before Nita's swift gun and the keen knife of Ram Singh. As he leaped into the tonneau, Ram Singh whipped the Daimler out into the traffic. Wentworth dropped back against the cushions and laughed sharply. He turned to Nita van Sloan. Her violet eyes were wide, her red lips pursed in anger. She still held the automatic with which she had shot her assailant and she let it sag to her knee with a slight shudder, smiled wanly into Wentworth's eyes. It was not the first time she had killed, but it always shook her.... She threw it off bravely.

"It looks as if our luncheon is being postponed," she said, smiling.

Wentworth's lips curved in answer. It was like strong drink to have this gallant woman beside him. "Jenkyns will be disappointed," he agreed. "He's been busy in the kitchen for hours."

Nita's hand went to Wentworth's arm and he closed his own over it, his eyes peering ahead once more. Ram Singh was wriggling the powerful Daimler through traffic at incredible speed, but the fugitive sedan managed to keep its lead. Wentworth caught up the speaking tube.

"Let them think they've lost us," he ordered, "but keep the trail I saw, O Ram Singh, that thy knife gained honor again!" He had lapsed into Ram Singh's native Punjabi for the last phrase and he saw the Sikh's shoulders straighten with pride. The Hindu was a tower of strength in Wentworth's many battles.

Wentworth relaxed again, confident that Ram Singh would perform the task assigned to him. He gazed into the warm depths of Nita's eyes. The smile on her full lips was wonderfully sweet.

"I shall have to feed you very soon," Nita said gravely. "You're trying to devour me with your eyes." She laughed, but with a touch of sadness, as there always must be in all their happiness. She knew why his eyes were hungry, why bitterness must always touch them. Death had been very close a few moments ago for all that they had made light of it, and death might lie in their path no further away than the next corner. She tried not to think of that, tried, too, to forget that probably she and Dick would never marry. No longer than a fortnight ago, she and Dick had stood together at the altar. Wentworth had foresworn his work—and word had came that the Fly had struck. Wentworth's mouth had gone grim as he stood there beside his bride—to-be. He had forced his lips to smile, had lifted a shoulder in a shrug.

"The Fly?" he said casually. "He means nothing to me."

He had pledged Nita that never again would the Spider seek his prey—and he intended to keep that promise. The moment had been incomparably sweet to Nita. She had savored it to the full—and had put it from her. With a smile, she had sent the lover who might never be more than that back into the battle. Never again would she flinch from the task he had set. If the end must come at the hands of his enemies, it would find them side by side.… Nita drew a little closer to Wentworth. *Side by side.…*

WENTWORTH THREW her a quick smile, then his eyes went back to the sedan they trailed. He drew his automatics and filled the partly emptied clips, saw that they were ready. He had hopes that this pursuit would lead him to some hideout of the Fly. What he would do then he did not know, but one thing was sure: The Fly must die before he gained still greater ascendency over the Underworld. Already, his power must be enormous.…

The speed of the pursuit had slackened and it seemed clear that the men ahead did not know they still were followed. What brought Wentworth rigidly erect in his seat was the abrupt realization that the direction of the chase had changed and that the killers were bound downtown—toward New York's famous financial district, where the richest banks of the world were situated! There could be no mistake. Already, they were too far southward in Manhattan to make any other destination possible. There was nothing save docks and office buildings, a few Syrian tenements. Wentworth whipped about.

"Nita, you must drop out. Phone the police that I think the Fly is about to raid a downtown bank." He rapped on the glass.

Ram Singh swerved the Daimler to the curb and Wentworth jerked open the door. Nita did not hesitate, though her lips were pressed together tightly. She gave Dick a twisted smile as he sprang past her with no more than a hand upon her arm for farewell. The Daimler leaped forward. For a moment, Nita watched. Her vision blurred. She pulled her head down and went blindly toward a tobacco shop to find a phone. She collided with some one, muttered an apology, but when she tried to go on, a hand gripped her arm painfully....

"Why, Nita," said a man's jeering voice. "This is indeed a surprise!"

Her head pulled up sharply. The man was a complete stranger to her, but his hard, leering eyes told her clearly that these were the men of the Fly! Nita's lips flew open. The man's eyes tightened. "Let me present my friend, Bull," he said. "That's short for Bullseye, because that's what he always hits."

Nita's head whipped about and she saw a dapper, small man bow jerkily. His eyes were black and mildly amused. His hands were in his coat pockets and those pockets bulged much too large for mere fists. He stepped to her side. "Let's take a walk," he said, and in his voice, too, was quiet amusement.

Nita's eyes flew about her wildly, but no one noticed this apparently friendly meeting. If she cried out, men might stare curiously, but no more. There were no police nearby. No help for it, but to submit to capture and hope that her chance would come later.... She was ushered smoothly to a waiting automobile which leaped instantly forward and Nita saw then how this had happened. There had been more than one of the Fly's cars on Fifth Avenue when she and Dick had been attacked. This second car had followed Wentworth while he trailed the killers. She was close to tears of vexation and despair, but she held her head high and there was even a faint smile on her lips. She could

48

The sedan hit a fire hydrant, bounced sideways
and knocked down a lamp-post!

not permit these hirelings of a butcher to see that the Spider's mate was worried....

While the gangster car, with Nita a prisoner, sped after him, Wentworth's attention was wholly centered on the men that he followed. He counted on Nita to phone his friend, Commissioner Kirkpatrick, of the police, the warning of what impended. He leaned tensely forward, trying to discover in advance just which bank was the target of the Fly's men. If he could do that and get fresh word to Kirkpatrick....

Abruptly, the car ahead whirled from broad West Street and shot up a side lane toward Broadway. Without an order, Ram Singh sent the Daimler racing forward at mounting speed. Wentworth uttered a low cry. The Bank of New York! Of all the financial institutions in the city, the Bank of New York carried the largest cash reserve and it was two blocks farther east along the street these men traveled. The Fly picked well!

Wentworth shot open the glass panel behind Ram Singh. "Wreck them!" he ordered sharply.

THE DAIMLER was off like a thoroughbred from the barrier. In half a block, it was crowding the tail of the gangster car. Ram Singh slammed into second gear, trod the gas pedal and rammed the sedan with a concussion like dynamite.

The gang car swerved, ploughed into a parked machine. The Fly's men did not wait to investigate. They flung to the pavement, plunged into the crowds upon the sidewalks. Wentworth let them go. He did not know what part they played in the Fly's plans, but at least this cog was stripped bare of its teeth....

The powerful engine of the Daimler was driving it steadily

forward. The sedan was wedged out of the way. A quick spurt backward, a wrench at the wheel and Ram Singh was racing on upgrade toward Broadway, toward the corner where the Bank of New York reared its solid mass.

Wentworth was still a half block away when the brazen alarm gong outside the bank burst into a frantic clanger. Before it had fairly started, a sedan spurted across the mouth of the street, heading up Broadway. A sub-machine gun cackled from its window. A woman who stood talking to a man on the corner had frozen at the sound of the gong. As the gun blasted she leaped up on tiptoes, grasping the man's arms, then both of them crumpled to the pavement. The woman's back was embroidered with red-rimmed holes. The man's face had been blown away. Five other persons fell before Wentworth's Daimler roared around the corner.

He was just in time to see the fleeing auto whirl a corner. Halfway to that corner, the Daimler yawed wildly as a small coupé started sharply out from the curb. There was a ripping crash. The coupé was hurled back into its slot in the parking line, but Ram Singh could not recover control quickly enough to follow behind the fugitives. Wentworth, peering back, saw the driver of the coupé leap from his seat and sprint away down Broadway. He lifted his gun, squeezed. The man fell. One trick of the Fly had failed!

His elation was short-lived. As the Daimler took the next corner eastward, he saw a second sedan with bellowing guns come racing up Broadway. From a side street, another lunged; off to westward, Wentworth could make out the chatter of still more guns. Damnation! The district was full of the men of the Fly! And where were the police? Surely, there had been time since Nita's warning. Police plans were laid so that within three minutes of an alarm, the financial section could be flooded with men, with armored motorcycles mounting machine guns, with squad cars loaded with men bearing riot guns and rifles. A small worry began to gnaw at the back of his brain. Why hadn't that alarm been given?

Broadway was left behind and the Daimler was sprinting eastward, crashing through stalled lanes of traffic. Ram Singh swung once to the sidewalk where machine gun bullets had spilled dead men, rounded a block in the street, and raced on. They had almost reached South Street before Wentworth heard the first police siren. He saw a car with spitting guns flash past the cross-street's end, and a moment later a police coupé shot into sight in its wake. One officer's revolver was speaking in slow, spaced rhythm. Wentworth had a glimpse of the bold lettering on the coupé's side, then the whole moving picture vanished northward….

"Cut back to Broadway!" Wentworth snapped. That car was trailed. There was no use in his joining the chase when there were so many other loads of killers racing amok through the district. As always, the Fly had been devastatingly clever in his conspiracy. In this multiplicity of scattered attacks, a half-dozen murder cars racing with blazing guns through the streets, police could, not concentrate their efforts, and the chances that they would close with the car which carried the loot were remote. Probably, that car would not even carry gunmen, but would cruise quietly away from the district, or else park in a side street nearby until the excitement had ended. The Fly might easily escape by subway with a grip full of loot....

"Faster!" Wentworth snapped. "Back to the bank!" Kirkpatrick would be there and from him must come the orders which would close the gaps that Wentworth's keen brain found. The Daimler flashed across William Street and a leaden hail hammered on the windows of the left side. They frosted over, but stopped the bullets. Ram Singh spun the steering wheel and the tires howled as they gripped the pavement in a sharp turn to the right. Wentworth had had no chance to speak, but he had reached forward to tap Ram Singh's right shoulder. No words had been necessary. While the car still rocked as it straightened out, the drum-roll of fire switched to the Daimler's right hand side. Wentworth cranked open a small gun port. He was deadly calm, but it was the quietness of rage. At last he was to have a chance to strike at the men who slew so wantonly....

ONLY ONE gun from the Fly's murder car was directed on Wentworth. Others swept the sidewalks to right and left. A newsboy cowered behind a lifted armful of papers and lead chewed through the pulp, hurled him kicking to the pavement. The litter of papers covered him, but from beneath their edges there crept thickening threads of red. A man dressing a store window stood staring, his mouth agape, a woman's brilliant frock in his hand. The window dissolved into silver powder. The dress whipped in the air like a flag. It was the man's death convulsion. These things Wentworth saw kaleidoscopically as the two cars raced side by side up narrow William Street.

53

Wentworth's first shot smashed the machine gun against the chest of the man who fired it, drove him backward to the floor. His second tore through the eyes of the driver, slashing in from the side, obliterating the bridge of his nose. He screamed horribly, jerking his hands to his face, and the gang car swung in a wide circle to the left. The Daimler's brakes took hold barely in time. Another killer tried to snatch at the wheel of his car, but he was too late. The sedan hit a fireplug, twisted sideways and snapped off a light post, jounced there with the three hundred pound pressure of the bursted water main hammering upward through its bottom.

"To the bank," Wentworth told Ram Singh. His voice rasped harshly in his throat. The car rolled forward.

The Spider's face was drained of all blood. Coolly, he reloaded his automatics, and his hands did not tremble, but there was a surging turmoil within him. That poor newsboy with his pitiful shroud of papers, that gay young couple whose nuptial bed was the cold, blood-washed pavement of Broadway.... The air was shivering with a furious crescendo of sirens and through a thickening stream of police cars, Wentworth made his way toward the Bank of New York. Everywhere the streets told a tale of wanton murder. Once more, a tragic massacre had covered the steps of the Fly.

Somberly, Wentworth counted more than twenty dead in the few short blocks he traversed. When he sprang from the Daimler a quarter block from the bank, age seemed suddenly to sit upon his face. Harsh lines bit into his cheeks beside his mouth

and there were moments, he seemed to have taken on years....
A policeman on guard at the bank door saluted him by name.

"Commissioner's inside, sir," he said respectfully.

They knew Richard Wentworth in the police force, knew him
for a trusted friend of the Commissioner. If they had suspected
that he was the Spider, there might have been a different sort
of salute, thundering guns whose bullets would pierce his flesh!
He passed two more guards before he strode into the presence
of Commissioner Kirkpatrick.

KIRKPATRICK STOOD in the middle of the lobby of
the rifled bank and on the floor about him were five still figures
covered in the merciful white shroud that the emergency wagons
always carried. At Wentworth's crisp step, the Commissioner's
head came up sharply, frosty blue eyes alert. A stiff smile stirred
his lips. These two had met on the scenes of a hundred tragedies,
but rarely had death conjured up such pictures as this.

"The Fly has surpassed himself," Kirkpatrick's voice came
forth clipped and strained. "Already there have been reported
forty-seven dead in the streets. That fiend out of hell! I'll...."
His hoarse anger choked him. He trembled with it, then fought
himself to calmness. "Know anything that will help, Dick?"

Wentworth's lips twisted as he told swiftly what he had seen
and done. In times like these, he and Kirkpatrick could work side
by side. In peaceful days, they were warmest friends, but Kirkpatrick was very sure that Wentworth was the Spider. There had
been days when the entire police force of the city hounded him
with orders—to bring him in, dead or alive—and always Went-

worth had proved that he could not possibly be the Spider… But now they must work together.

"… And block the subways," he finished his suggestions, which were transmuted into orders even as he talked. "Have you had a report from a twenty-fourth precinct police coupé which trailed a gangster car up South Street?"

Kirkpatrick's long-fingered hand rose to his pointed black mustache, brushed first one side, then the other. He was frowning. He snapped a query at an officer nearby and received a negative answer. No car had been reported trailing a gangster sedan….

Wentworth stared at Kirkpatrick with his blue-gray eyes sharply excited. "Where is the twenty-fourth precinct?" he demanded. "In the west Nineties, isn't it?"

Kirkpatrick nodded slowly. "That's exactly it," he said. "Why should a car from that far uptown be down here on the trail of that gangster car before any of the other police had time…?" He broke off, slapped a fist into his palm. "By God, that was…."

Wentworth nodded grimly. "That was the Fly, beyond a doubt, in a stolen or faked police coupé. And, also beyond a doubt, one of those two cars carried the loot of this bank!"

Kirkpatrick whirled from him. His orders crackled with the speed of high frequency electric sparks, but Wentworth was silent. All this was useless now. It had been fully fifteen, probably twenty, minutes since he had seen that police car. The Fly had made good his escape, abandoned the coupé… It was damnably clever. He had had the benefits of a police siren in clearing the way for his flight, and the blazing guns of the car which he apparently pursued, actually his convoy, would protect him in case of discovery....

Kirkpatrick was back again. "A pity we didn't have more warning," he said, "but I doubt that even then we would have penetrated that trick in time to stop the Fly."

Wentworth's head had jerked up at the words. The small worry that had popped into his brain at the slowness of police response came back to him again and gripped his heart with icy fingers. He stepped close and seized Kirkpatrick's arm. He had to squeeze out words and they, had a strained, harsh sound.

"Kirk, how... did you get the alarm?" He thought: Nita! Good God, *Nita!*

Kirkpatrick stared at him curiously. "The alarm system," he said. "When the gong went off outside...."

Wentworth's fingers bit deeply into the arm. He strained forward, eyes questioning Kirkpatrick's, then his hand dropped. He straightened and drew in a slow, hissing breath.

"The Fly has Nita," he whispered.

Kirkpatrick cried. "What, Dick? What about Nita?"

Wentworth explained heavily how Nita had left the car to phone a warning. "There can't be any other explanation," he said slowly. "If Nita did not telephone you, it was because she was prevented. Only the Fly could have... stopped her."

Kirkpatrick did not attempt to deny it. He whipped about to shout an order, stopped as a man in the uniform of a Western Union messenger came limping across the lobby. Wentworth watched him come and a pain throbbed in his heart. Somehow he knew, even before Kirkpatrick ripped open the envelope, what it would contain.

"For you!" Kirkpatrick said, his voice shaky.

Wentworth read the yellow slip that quivered in Kirkpatrick's fingers. It was signed "the Fly." It read:

"Nita came into my parlor, Spider!"

CHAPTER 6
A DANGEROUS GAME

WENTWORTH GAZED fixedly at the taunting message of the Fly. His lips twitched once, he moved his shoulders heavily. He was aware of Kirkpatrick shouting orders that the telegram be traced, but neither of them expected any success from that line of inquiry.

"The Fly never dared do such a thing as this before," Kirkpatrick said harshly. "We'll break him. We'll destroy his every man...."

Wentworth smiled slightly. "How—?" he demanded, quietly. "If you don't mind, I'm going home." He turned away. His thoughts swung in crazy circles. The premonitions which had harassed him were fulfilled to the utmost. To be sure, it was not the first time that Nita had been kidnaped by his enemies, but repetition never dulled the edge of his despair. Too often he had snatched his loved one back from the very brink of death. Ultimately, he must fail, and the Fly was the most clever criminal he had ever engaged. He could not lift the black veil from his thoughts....

Wentworth brought up short as he saw two uniformed men dragging a prisoner toward Kirkpatrick. The man seemed more infuriated at their touch than reluctant to confront the Commissioner, but at any rate he was resisting violently. Abruptly, Wentworth recognized the prisoner. *Charles Holland!* The policemen held him rigidly before Kirkpatrick. Holland lifted his head in proud defiance. He gripped the upper half of a broken cane....

Wentworth made his way after Holland. He had no inkling as to the reason for the arrest, but the mere sight of that man on the scene of this atrocious crime was enough to arouse suspicion. His brother, that earlier Fly, had frequently used the trick of wearing a disguise during a crime, then reverting to his own identity and showing himself to the police. Was it possible that Charles Holland was following the same tactics?

Wentworth drew near enough to hear the policeman tell of finding Holland. "He was up on the fifteenth floor, looking through offices. A girl got scared and phoned up headquarters, so we took him."

Kirkpatrick nodded, "All right. Go back to your post."

The cop's heavy face worked. "Shall I iron him, Commissioner?"

Kirkpatrick shook his head, his frosty blue eyes holding Holland's. The Commissioner was easily fifteen years older than the other, as the gray at his temples attested. There were grim lines about his mouth corners and his eyes were tired. They could be very kindly; just now they were grimly quizzical.

The cop said, "Commissioner, you better let me iron him. He took a poke at me and, cheez, did I see stars!"

59

CLAIBORNE LEE

DR. LEAMING

GARY COX

"Back to your post," Kirkpatrick ordered quietly and the policeman curved his mouth corners down, lifted his brows, resigning all responsibility. He walked away with his partner and Holland only shrugged his shoulders, pulled down his coat sleeves. Anger had flushed the fresh color of his cheeks. Kirkpatrick smiled slightly.

"You shouldn't have hit Morgan," he reproved. "It's a wonder he didn't use his stick on you. He'd have been justified, you know."

Holland laughed shortly, and lifted the broken cane. "He tried to, but I had my stick. I agreed to go with them and then they grabbed me and roughed me along. You should teach your men manners, Kirkpatrick."

"Where they work," Kirkpatrick said quietly, "manners are considered a weakness. Do you want to explain your presence here or at headquarters—later?"

HOLLAND STIFF-ENED under the crisp lash of the words. "I was not aware that explanation was called for. I had business in the building...."

"Business of what sort?"

Wentworth laid a hand on Kirkpatrick's arm. The Commissioner was distraught. He would not, under ordinary circumstances, handle Holland in this way.

"Kirk," he said, "I'll be responsible for Holland, if you like."

Kirkpatrick eyed Wentworth, fingered his mustache, then nodded abruptly. If Dick wanted the man, there was a reason behind it, and a sound one. He nodded.

Wentworth motioned to the man. "Holland," he said quietly,

CHARLES HOLLAND

LOU COX

FOSTER SHERWOOD

"the Fly has kidnapped by fiancée, and I thought you might give me a little help in tracing her."

"I know nothing of the Fly," Holland retorted testily.

"I'm willing to believe that," Wentworth conceded. "Would you come with me, please? I'm going to my apartment."

"I have no choice, and you know it. I won't run from the police and for the present you're my custodian."

Wentworth made no answer to that. Holland was fiery and young and his behavior seemed sincere. It was true that he had a chip on his shoulder, but that was an outgrowth from the fact that his brother had gone outside the law. Wentworth bowed Holland into the Daimler, told Ram Singh to drive home slowly. He sank back in his corner of the seat and sat staring straight ahead of him. He felt like a fighter who has taken too many heavy blows below the heart, tired, with the spring gone out of his legs. Yes, below the heart... *Nita.* He closed his eyes and presently began to talk that way, his voice muffled with fatigue.

"I'm told, Holland, that last night, during the raid on your masquerade party, you didn't kill the Fly when you had an opportunity...."

Holland's voice exploded out of him. "He called me his brother! It sounded like... Jack."

"Didn't you bury Jack?"

"I don't... know," Holland was clearly worried. "The body was pretty badly mangled and had landed on its head. I'll tell you now that we found no saber wound on the body."

Wentworth whipped erect, his eyes narrowed on Holland's face. "This is painful to you, I know," he said, "but my thrust

62

touched here." He tapped his finger above the collar bone on the left side. "An eight-inch thrust there would have pierced the heart. Four inches would have severed the aorta. I could not swear to the depth of penetration, but you know the feel of steel in flesh…."

Holland's face was white. This was his brother that they talked about, this was the man who had slain him, or at least run a sword into his body. Wentworth had been in his own identity when he had sabered Jack Holland, though there were Spider seals upon many of the Fly's companions. A tremor shook Wentworth's prisoner, but he held on to himself. It was moments before he could speak….

"There was no such wound on the body," he said shakily. "I inspected it closely, trying to make sure of identification. Naturally, I did not reveal my doubts. If Jack had escaped… Well, my investigations proved that another man had fallen from a window in the building. He was executed in that way at Jack's order, I was told. But, Mr. Wentworth, are you sure… the saber penetrated?"

WENTWORTH CLOSED his eyes, leaned back to think. It was clear that Charles Holland wanted to believe his brother dead. He tried to remember that windy moment when, on a ladder bridging a gulf between two apartment building roofs, the Fly had hurled himself forward, close to the ladder, in a violent lunge; Wentworth had parried the lunge with a stop-thrust, driven at the base of the throat. The Fly had instantly plunged from the ladder, but he might have been overbalanced by his lunge… Wentworth opened his eyes.

"I used to be sure, Holland," he said, "but now, when I think of it, I can't be."

The men were silent through minutes while the Daimler wove its way northward. They were on Fifth Avenue. In a half-dozen blocks, they would be at Wentworth's apartment. He stirred himself. A resolution was forming within him. If he succeeded in freeing Nita from this dilemma, he would make sure that she was never involved again. How he would arrange that…? He smiled sardonically. How many times had he made that same oath—and broken it!… Through years of constant, secret warfare, he had put the people he thanklessly served before everything, even before Nita, and she had rarely complained. And, once more, now, he must do that. The Fly would communicate with him with a demand that he drop out of the fight, on pain of Nita's death. He would refuse, even though it doomed Nita. He couldn't do anything else, and Nita… Would he be able to snatch her once more from destruction? He must, he must….

"Holland, the girl called Lou, who was shot last night," Wentworth said. "Would you mind telling me her name?"

"I would!" Holland said sharply. "She wasn't badly hurt, a flesh wound under the arm, and I won't permit her to be prosecuted."

Wentworth nodded, as if it did not matter. "I see, and who is Gary?"

Holland's hands gripped Wentworth's arm. "In heaven's name, Mr. Wentworth, what prompts these questions?" he cried. "I tell you that Lou and her brother are entirely innocent It's just that the Fly has got hold of the kid… You must believe me. They're innocent."

Wentworth lifted his shoulders slightly; but beneath his lowered lids, his blue-gray eyes were speculative. A girl named Lou and her brother, Gary, in the Fly's power. And Charles Holland was in love with the girl.... The Daimler drew to a halt and Ram Singh sprang to the pavement, flung wide the door.

"I'd be pleased to have you come up, Holland," he said, "but if you wish, you may go. I gave my word that you would be available when ready. I know that you will respect that promise and hold yourself ready for Mr. Kirkpatrick."

Holland had alighted. He turned to Wentworth with a smile. "You're an all right guy," he said eagerly. "I'm beginning to understand why Kirkpatrick trusts you... and why other people hate you." He hesitated. "I'm going to call on Lou. I can't object now to telling you her name because I know you won't misuse the knowledge. She's Lou Cox. Gary is her brother. They're quite well-to-do, even wealthy, in their own right, and they live with their uncle and guardian...."

Wentworth's face cleared. "Of course," he said. "They're Foster Sherwood's wards. I knew that those names were familiar. You're right, Holland, I won't misuse the information, but I'm going to find that young man and have a talk with him. Gary Cox."

Holland said fervently, "I wish to God you would!

He stepped back, bowed and lifted his hat, as men do on the Continent as a mark of extreme respect. He pivoted and was about to march off along the street. Wentworth stopped him with a hail, smiling slightly as he pointed to the stub of a broken cane which Holland still carried.

"Don't you want me to dispose of that for you?" he said. "It looks rather ridiculous."

HOLLAND LAUGHED, handed it over to Wentworth with hurried thanks, and strode on. He did not notice that Wentworth gripped the cane very carefully by its broken end, so as not to disturb any palm prints that, might be upon its head. Ram Singh closed the door and stood beside Wentworth, waiting for orders.

"Missie sahib has been kidnaped by the Fly," Wentworth told him flatly. His acquisition of the broken cane had been almost instinctive. His mind bore heavily on the misfortune of Nita…. He saw fierceness leap into the Sikh's eyes. Devotion to women did not come traditionally to this Hindu, but he had fought under Nita's orders and had found her braver even than the women of his own Punjab hills. As his master's mate, she would deserve his most devoted service, even if she were not so strong in her own right. Ram Singh's hand went to the knife hilt at his sash.

"Park the car and come after me," Wentworth told him. "I'm waiting for word, either from the Fly or from Jackson."

He went heavily to his penthouse, shed coat and hat and handed the broken cane carefully to Jenkyns with instructions to develop the prints on it. He had not looked at Jenkyns while he spoke, but abruptly seeing his face, Wentworth felt hope spring up within him. Jenkyns smiled like that for only one person in the world….

"Miss Nita…?" Wentworth whispered.

"Yes, Master Dick," said Jenkyns, "Miss Nita and a Mr. Claiborne Lee are waiting for you, sir."

His heart singing, Wentworth strode through the hall. Nita van Sloan was seated on the low, long davenport that faced the brick fireplace. Before her, Claiborne Lee stood easily, a wine glass lifted in salute. Their smiles held comradeship, a mutual respect. They had not heard his entrance....

"To the bravest, and the most beautiful woman I have ever met," said Claiborne Lee, bowing. Nita laughed, her contralto a sweet bell note.

"You have your own share of bravery, Mr. Lee," she answered him.

Wentworth stood looking at them, his eyes burning. He guessed what had happened. This talk of bravery could mean only, that Lee had rescued her from the Fly. His lips pressed thinly together. How had Lee managed to be on the scene, why had he undertaken the rescue? So far as Wentworth was aware, Lee did not know Nita and it was improbable that the kidnaping had been spectacular or even obvious. Foolish to suspect Claiborne Lee on such little evidence, if he could call it that, but Wentworth had realized that "hunches" were frequently the functioning of the subconscious mind.... What he determined on was inspirational. For this one time, at least, he could protect Nita and, if Lee were guilty, plant a spy in the heart of the enemy camp.... Nita would understand, her quick mind would grasp what he wanted.

FROM HIS position just inside the door, Wentworth spoke: "I see you returned safely from your little affair with the

Fly." There was a sneer and harshness in its syllables. Claiborne Lee's head whipped about. Nita started, then turned toward him. She came slowly to her feet as Wentworth strode across the room. She smiled, held out her hands to him….

"Dick," she said, "I want you to know Mr. Claiborne Lee." She hurriedly told the story of her seizure by the men of the Fly. "When their car was stopped by the next traffic light, Mr. Lee pulled up beside us, shot the driver and came straight at the other two men with his gun out. He used the side of the car for protection, killed another of them, and the third one tried to get away. But he shot him dead, too. He's almost as good a shot as you are, Dick."

Wentworth bowed coldly. "And a much braver man, I am sure. Would you mind, Lee, telling me just how you happened to be in the downtown district and why you killed your own men?"

Lee frowned. "I don't know what you're talking about, or why you are being so unmannerly," he said coldly. "But I shall certainly demand explanations when you are a little less distraught." He bowed.

"Miss van Sloan, are you staying, or may I see you home?"

Wentworth's hand reached out, caught the man's arm. He jerked him about so that their eyes met each other's with an almost solid impact. "I'll tell you what I mean, Lee," he said with metallic sharpness. "I mean that you are the man who directed the bandits at Holland's home last night and planned the looting of the Bank of New York today. You are the man who shot Lou Cox. In short, Mr. Lee, you are the Fly!"

Lee wrenched his arm free, stared coldly at Wentworth,

turned to Nita. "I'm afraid Mr. Wentworth has gone completely mad. I think it would be much better if you went with me."

"She will not!" Wentworth rasped. He made a deliberately awkward punch at Lee's face which the man easily evaded. He kept his face twisted into a furious frown, and would not look at Nita. Lee must not become suspicious of their simulated quarrel…. Nita's hand touched Wentworth's arm.

"Dick, boy," she said gently, "what's the matter? You surely don't mean what you said to Mr. Lee. I know…."

Wentworth wrenched his arm free of her hand. "Were you really kidnaped by the Fly?" he sneered, "or is this just some story of yours to trick me?"

Nita flinched back, the pure oval of her face very pale, her eyes startled and hurt.

Claiborne Lee said, "I really must insist that you go with me, Miss van Sloan."

"By all means," Wentworth sneered. "By all means. Perhaps his bravery will protect you!"

He strode from the room. Jenkyns stood in the hallway, his face strained and amazed. Wentworth stopped—before him, shouting, "Get them out of here, you doddering old fool! Get them out of here before I kill them both!"

HE STORMED along the hall, reached his own suite and rushed inside. He closed and locked the door, stood with his legs braced apart, his breath coming sharply. He was frowning. Damn it, Nita had seemed so startled and hurt! Surely, she understood his purpose, that the quarrel was simulated. He had had to make it forceful, even to bellowing at poor old

Jenkyns. He smiled briefly at the memory of Jenkyns' amazed face, but his amusement quickly died. Nita *had* to understand. He could not communicate with her, for if Lee were the Fly he would suspect a false quarrel, would be on the lookout for secret conversations…. Oh, damn it, this was….

The tapping at the door was very gentle, "Dick, boy," Nita called. "Come here and talk with me."

Wentworth whirled toward the door, his jaw tightly clenched, his hands knotted at his sides. This was harder than that other, but Lee would be watching. He must force himself still to simulate anger. If only he could be sure that Nita understood! He swallowed twice before he could force out words.

"Get the hell out of here!" he shouted. "Leave my house and don't come back."

Silence then. Wentworth stood, straining his ears, leaning forward, his eyes peering as if he would see through that barrier which separated him from the woman he loved. The silence kept on and on. Dimly, Wentworth thought he heard a door slam. With a gasp that was dry and hard in his throat, he started toward the door of his room. He forced himself to remain inside. Of course, Nita understood. It was foolish of him to think even for a moment that she could take him seriously. She knew how deeply he loved her, and….

The startled, hurt face of Nita arose before his eyes to mock him. He walked slowly back across the room, glimpsed himself in the mirror and moved closer, staring at his reflection, the creases that each month etched more deeply about his lips, the stipple of premature silver there above his temples. He had always driven himself to the right course regardless of what it cost and the iron of his will was there in the lines that marked the frequent compression of his mouth. He smiled at himself with a quizzical lift of his brows. Agonizing, eh? Playing at melodramatics. But, damn it, life was made up of melodramatics.... It was going to be hard to fight this battle without the strong support of Nita at his side, still harder to keep up the pretense of bitterness and anger. A dry, hard sound forced itself up out of his throat. He changed that sound to a laugh, kept on laughing, laughing....

CHAPTER 7
IS NITA A TRAITOR?

IT WAS two hours before Wentworth left his room, and his face was so sternly forbidding that old Jenkyns, who had served Wentworth's father before him, thought better of speaking to him. Ram Singh stood with his shoulders close to the wall, arms folded across his white tunic. His eyes followed Wentworth ceaselessly, but he did not speak. The ways of western men with western women were past his understanding....

Wentworth moved restlessly about the drawing room. He had a driving urge for decisive, slashing action. As yet, there was no opportunity for that, but when it came....

"Has Jackson called?" The harshness of his voice surprised Wentworth's own ear. His eyes burned on Jenkyns'.

"No, Master Dick," Jenkyns said quietly. "Master, I saw tears in Miss Nita's eyes when she left."

Wentworth reached Jenkyns with three long strides. "Jenkyns," he said harshly. "You've been with me a long time, and you should know—"

Old Jenkyns looked at his young master with miserable eyes. There could be no question of his devotion, but this was terribly wrong, this anger against Miss Nita. His bowed shoulders straightened, his silvery head came up. He would have defied Wentworth then, but the telephone bell rang.... Jenkyns hesitated, then his shoulders drooped and he turned away. He came back slowly.

"Jackson on the phone, Master Dick."

Wentworth did not wait for the portable to be brought to him, but strode rapidly along the hall to the butler's pantry. "Yes, Jackson?" He listened to the rapid words of the man who was as much his friend as his servant. They had served together in the World War, Sergeant Jackson and Major Wentworth... "I'll join you in ten minutes."

He hung up, sent his shout to Ram Singh ringing ahead of him, caught hat and coat from Jenkyns' hands. There was a smile hard on his lips, his eyes were narrowed and bitter. The Spider was on the warpath. God help whatever men interposed between him and the Fly.

The Daimler surged with power as Wentworth gave swift instructions. "I told Jackson we'd be there in ten minutes," Wentworth said quietly. This rush of reckless speed, this evasion of traffic lights was his answer. He was well served.... In his quandary over Nita, Wentworth thought briefly that it would be better were the Spider to fight his battles alone. Gallant men he had had beyond a doubt, but their attachment to him could never bring them other than death in the end. Both Jackson and Ram Singh had been wounded a half-dozen times in his service. SUCH THOUGHTS would not do. He forced himself to consider the information that Jackson had given him. Gary Cox lived with his guardian, Foster Sherwood, who was a young man for the responsibility of handling the millions of the Cox heirs, younger than Wentworth. They occupied an ancient house near Long Island Sound in Pelham. The house had a history; it had been built on the site of an old-time tavern known as the Smugglers' Rest....

Wentworth's mind would not concentrate on the possibilities of the situation. He was considering falteringly the chance that Foster Sherwood might be stealing from the estate of the two Cox heirs, that he had driven his ward and nephew into crime with a view to being rid of him.... Hell, could Sherwood be the Fly? He was able with a rapier, Wentworth knew. He ridiculed his thoughts. Damnable that every person he knew must fall under suspicion.... Wearily, he took up his duties....

Wentworth caught up the speaking tube that communicated with Ram Singh. Always, when he went into danger, he left a record of his progress in the case that, in event of disaster, would be turned over to Kirkpatrick. Formerly, Nita had served him in that capacity, but he dared not communicate with her.... His lips were awry as he began talking to Ram Singh....

"In the safe that you know of in my room," he said, "is a moulage cast of a man's palm print. I am reasonably sure that this is the palm print of the Fly—" he explained his reasons for think-

73

ing so, the adventures at Holland's masquerade. "On my return from the masquerade, I sent Jackson to determine the name of the girl who was shot, to learn what person connected with her was named Gary and to find and trail that person. He has followed her brother, named Gary Cox, to a doctor's office on the East Side. We are going there now. Gary Cox went into the doctor's office a half hour ago and, when Jackson went into the waiting room, he was not in sight. Keep this carefully in mind. It shall be your duty to preserve your life and to carry this message to Kirkpatrick if misfortune should befall me. Understand?"

Ram Singh's usually prompt *"Han, sahib!"* was delayed. In Punjabi, he asked slowly, "Does this mean, my master, that thy servant may not fight beside thee?"

Wentworth rasped out a repetition of his order and Ram Singh was silent. This was not his master's manner, to order him harshly and without explanation to become a coward! Wentworth bowed his head, inspected his automatics with dry eyes as he checked the clips, the chamber and the cock, threw on the safety before restoring them to their holsters. Even Ram Singh's bravery did not stir him as formerly. If misfortune should befall me...."

His lips set thinly. He opened a compartment in the back of the front seat and took out a notebook, unscrewed a fountain pen cap and wrote slow and painful words across the white paper. This car, along with everything else he possessed, would go to Nita in the event of his death. She would find this notebook....

IT WAS not like the Spider to go into battle with such despair

74

in his heart, but even that fact did not make him falter. It had been many years since the thought of death had disturbed him.... The car slowed to the curb and a man with a wide stocky body stepped from a dark doorway to meet it. At Wentworth's curt invitation, he entered the back seat.

"You beat your time by two minutes, Major," he said. "The lad hasn't come out yet."

Wentworth nodded. "Go into the office and wait for the doctor. Ram Singh will watch at the window. I'll come in later in disguise. If you don't see Gary Cox by that time, we'll take the doctor and ask some questions."

Jackson's wide jaws ceased with a grin. "Yes, Major!"

Ram Singh glided from the front seat of the car and strode away beside Jackson. Wentworth drew the curtains of the car and pressed a button beneath the edge of the left half of the seat. The seat slid slowly forward, revolved and revealed a closely hung wardrobe, a mirror brilliantly lighted by a ring of neon tubes beneath which was a make-up tray. With skillful fingers then, Wentworth set to work to disguise his face. Under his deft fingers, his nose became beaked and predatory; the skin over his cheekbones tautened in sallowness, the mouth became lipless.... In short, the face of the Spider grew over his own. It was swiftly done. Long practice had done that for him. His hat was a light brown fedora and he wore a threadbare overcoat rather than the black cape and hat of the Spider. It was not yet his purpose to terrify. That might come later.... He hoped it would.

Wentworth's lips had a thinness that was not all due to disguise as he limped across the street toward where the doctor's lighted sign glowed against the dusk. His shoulders were twisted awkwardly and it gave his carriage a singularly sinister aspect. As he entered the outer door, the four patients in the room glanced up toward him and Wentworth was struck immediately with the faces of two of them. They had the wary, shallow eyes of killers and their hands had the nervous habit of gunmen. They never strayed far from weapons. Jackson was in the seat nearest the door. He shook his head slightly to indicate that Gary Cox had not yet shown himself and Wentworth limped directly to the doctor, whose name, the sign had said, was Leaming.

"Dr. Leaming," Wentworth's voice was high and disagreeable. "Would you mind taking me next? I'm suffering awful pain in my back and I need relief. I must have relief! Do you hear? I must have relief." Wentworth lifted his hands, shaking them violently. His artificially pinched face was thrust forward. He was studying this Dr. Leaming closely. The man's face was smooth and round, the eyes might have been kindly behind horn-rimmed spectacles except for a cold light in their depths....

"I'm sorry, I can't do that," said Dr. Leaming. "If you'll just have a seat."

"Aw, let him in first, doc," Jackson broke in. "Can't you see the guy's in pain?"

"I must have relief!" Wentworth cried. Out of the corner of his eyes, he was watching the two men he had spotted as gunmen. They were sitting at rigid attention, hands in their gun pockets. What was their purpose here? Were they guards for this Leaming, or were they prospective patients as they pretended to be? Wentworth faced them, whining, "You don't mind if a man what's suffering goes in ahead of you? I know you don't. You're kind men. I can see it in—your faces. See, Doctor, they don't object...."

JACKSON WAS on his feet beside the doctor and, though Jackson's lips did not move, Wentworth saw abruptly that he had spoken, that his right hand was out of direct sight behind the doctor's back and that perspiration was standing out on the man's forehead.

"A-all right," he stuttered. "Come right in...."

He backed into his office. Wentworth followed him, and Jackson sat down again to keep watch on the two men whom Wentworth suspected. Wentworth followed the doctor and took his gun out at the same instant.

"Pardon the haste," he murmured, "but I must take every precaution, as you will understand when you learn my identity."

The doctor reeled into the seat behind his desk and lifted a wavering hand to his forehead. "I—I have no narcotics," he whispered, "and very little money."

"I'm inclined to doubt both statements," Wentworth replied suavely, "but I did not come here in quest of either article you mention. I came to...."

The doctor's round face lifted, a puzzled frown on the smooth forehead. The eyes were slowly widening. His shoulders cringed in the chair. "What, oh what do you want?" he cried.

Wentworth bent forward. "Where," he whispered, "is Gary Cox?"

There was no answering flair in the doctor's eyes and Wentworth saw that the name meant absolutely nothing to Leaming.

77

Yet it wasn't possible that Jackson was mistaken and there were those two men on guard in the ante-room. What this meant was that Dr. Leaming had acted without knowing the man's name. It all had some definite criminal significance....

"He's quite young and very handsome. What message did you give him?" Wentworth asked next.

Dr. Leaming had got back a modicum of courage when the first question had shown that Wentworth was ignorant of his work. Wentworth saw that and smiled—somberly. He reached out his right hand and something that gleamed in it touched fleetingly the prescription pad that rested before the man. When his hand had returned to his side, something crimson glowed there against the white paper and Dr. Leaming rose to his feet with a muffled scream, backing frantically away from the *seal of the Spider* which stared up at him with its mocking threat of death.

"Don't kill me, Spider," babbled Dr. Leaming. "Don't kill me...!"

Wentworth's lipless mouth twisted in a smile of mockery. "Where is Gary Cox?" he demanded again.

"I don't know, Spider. For God's sake, I don't know the names of any of the men who come here. Any time one of them mentions the Fly and his own number, I give him a little prescription that's already written out, one for each number, and he goes out the back entrance of the apartment building. That's all I know...."

Wentworth held out his left hand. "Let me have all the

prescriptions that are written out, Dr. Leaming. If the Fly asks you about it, tell him that the Spider paid you a call...."

LEAMING SURRENDERED the prescriptions, and Wentworth glanced hastily at them. At first glance, they told him nothing. He said, "Good, now call in the man who held a gun at your back. After which we'll both go out through the back entrance. Remember, though, if you make a single hostile move...." Wentworth lifted the muzzle of his gun and Dr. Leaming cringed toward the door, called Jackson in with a strained voice. As Wentworth's man moved in, Wentworth whistled a few bars of a weird minor strain. It told Ram Singh that everything was all right, to go back to the car.... Two minutes later, the doctor having been strapped competently in his chair and gagged with his own adhesive tape, Wentworth and Jackson made their way out of the back entrance. They kept sharp lookout, but could find no trace of a hidden headquarters of the Fly. Wentworth did not seriously expect to find any, for it was pretty clear that the Fly used the doctor's office as a clearing place for orders to his men.

Wentworth posted Jackson to keep watch on the rear entrance and to follow either of the two men who left, or if they remained, to trail Dr. Leaming when next he went out. Ram Singh would keep similar lookout in front. And the Spider...? Wentworth smiled slightly. This was not the action he wished, but at least it would keep him busy....

"These prescriptions carry some sort of coded message," Wentworth announced briefly. "I shall wait in the

Daimler around the corner and try to decipher them. Communicate there."

In the Daimler, Wentworth drew a desk tray from the back of the seat ahead of him and spread the prescriptions under its hooded light. At first glance they were innocent enough, one for a sedative, another apparently some compound for a sick stomach, the third a liniment. Yet Wentworth was sure that somewhere in these scribbled formulas were messages to members of the Fly's band dealing with some new atrocity which he planned.

The Fly had proved that he could strike rapidly and with force. Here was none of the slow preparation that had characterized the previous visitation of the criminal who used that name. Last night, it had been the raid on Holland's masquerade, then two swift attacks upon the Spider and as close on the heels of the second as possible, the looting of the Bank of New York. Wentworth had every reason then to think that still another atrocity was being planned, that these slips of paper....

All three prescriptions had been signed by Leaming, and the names of the patients were there, too, with addresses. Wentworth's eyes narrowed abruptly. That address for one Oscar Schmidt, 765 East Fortieth street, was an impossibility. There was no such address. Could the code be hidden in those few brief numbers? Hurriedly, Wentworth examined the other prescriptions, inspecting names and addresses. He was desperate with the need for haste. Even while he puzzled over these anonymous slips, the Fly might be preparing to strike. The Spider knew the Fly well enough to be sure that the mere absence of three of his criminal aides would not interrupt his plans. He would arrange duplicate and even triplicate coverage....

Wentworth's attention was drawn sharply to the pepsin prescription, made out in a woman's name, a Riverside Drive address. Good God, it was Nita's address! This was madness. Could they be planning to strike again at the woman he loved! His lips shut grimly. Why shouldn't they? There was a way to make sure. He would seize the three who came for these prescriptions, force them to talk....

Wentworth slid from the car, stole through the thickened night to where he knew Ram Singh kept watch. He stood beside him in a darkened doorway. "Has anyone entered?" he asked softly.

"None yet, *sahib*," Ram Singh replied, "but a woman and a man come there at the corner...."

Wentworth's eyes shot where the Sikh indicated and his breath caught in his throat as he saw the woman. It wasn't possible, and yet, God knew, he should recognize that proud carriage of the head, that easy grace of movement.

"Sahib!" whispered Ram Singh, "it is..." His breath choked off as Wentworth closed his hand upon the Hindu's arm. He could no longer doubt, but perhaps she was not going to the doctor's office? He told himself that, but there was no belief in him. The woman and man came rapidly nearer, the sharp taps of her heels making staccato echoes along the street, the man's much slower and deliberate. They paused for a moment before the entrance of the doctor's office, looked at the gleaming sign, then ran up the steps and entered.... Wentworth's hand dropped from Ram

Singh's arm. He did not know the man, but he understood the address on the woman's prescription now, for the woman who had just entered the office of the Fly's go-between was... *Nita van Sloan!*

CHAPTER 8
THE SPIDER FINDS DESPAIR

FOR ONCE, surprise held Wentworth inactive. He stood in the shadowed doorway with Ram Singh and stared sightlessly at the door across the street into which Nita van Sloan had disappeared. What in the world did her presence here at this place mean? Who was this man? It was plain they had come to receive coded orders from the Fly....

Wentworth gnawed at his lip, gazed and gazed until his eyes were dazzled by the lighted doctor's sign. He could sense the impatience of Ram Singh and he thought with a twisted smile that even the Sikh must be wondering at his behavior toward the *missie sahib* whose orders he had been taught to accept as implicitly as the Spider's own. But he must do something.

"Wait here," he ordered Ram Singh harshly. "If the *missie sahib* comes out, follow her and phone back your report to Jenkyns. I'll call there...."

In the darkness, Wentworth caught the movement of the Sikh's abrupt salaam, cupped hands lifted to his turbaned head. Wentworth then strode toward the alleyway where Jackson kept watch. His feet hit the ground violently. Anger had him by the throat, anger at himself, at the thing he had possibly done to Nita.... Damn it, she should understand....

In the mouth of the alley, Wentworth paused, peering into the shadows that clustered thick against the fences, the walls of buildings. Somewhere here, Jackson should be keeping watch. He had been posted close to this end. Softly, Wentworth whistled the minor notes of their signal. He waited and there was no answer. Alarm stabbed sharply into the Spider's vitals. Where the devil was Jackson? Swiftly, Wentworth crept into the black, narrow defile of the alley, found the gate that was the back door of the doctor's office. He entered... and stumbled over a soft and yielding object.

With a curse, Wentworth dropped to his knees. He did not need his eyes to know—that this was Jackson. His swift fingers detected the uniform, found his throat pulse.... A breath of relief forced itself out of Wentworth's set lips. He was only unconscious. How had anyone managed to get close enough to that doughty warrior to overpower him? No way of telling until he regained consciousness, but his presence here meant one sure thing: the birds had flown. Nita...?

Wentworth sprang to his feet, dragging Jackson's weight across his shoulders in a fireman's lift He moved rapidly toward the office of the doctor. Leaming was gone, so were the two gunmen. The other legitimate patient was just stirring to consciousness. Bitter laughter shook Wentworth. He crossed to the window, signaled Ram Singh. It was his own weakness that had done this, his delay in deciding on action against Nita.

In a few minutes, Wentworth had the story. The patient,

having recovered, said that a good-looking woman had come in with a man—and told the other two men in the office that the place was watched. "She went to the office, found the doctor tied up—" The man swallowed hard—"She spun about, pointed to me and said 'Conk him!' One of them did, with a blackjack." JACKSON'S FACE was puzzled and ashamed. He kept glancing at Wentworth, then looking down at the floor. "Out with it," Wentworth told him grimly. "I know it was Miss Nita."

"You could of knocked me down with a feather,"

Jackson said humbly. "Miss Nita comes out into the alley and whistles the way you do. 'Jackson?' she whispers. Hell, I walked up to her and she let me have it. Blackjack, I think, sir."

"I rather imagine it wasn't a feather," Wentworth said drily. There was no real humor in him. His men were puzzled, their morale shaken as well it might be. How Nita had discovered that the house was watched, he had no idea, but she knew the Spider's methods very thoroughly. She would have known that it was Jackson he would place at the secret entrance where he would have to use discretion in his action. Ram Singh was equally brave, but he knew only one form of action, to obey or to kill. When in doubt, he killed....

Wentworth said heavily, "We'll have to change our signals. Both of you disregard any further orders from Miss Nita. She is not... our ally any longer. By the way, Jackson, did you know the third man with Miss Nita?"

Jackson started. "Yes, by God! I knew there was something I was trying to remember. That blackjack... It was Foster Sherwood, Major."

Wentworth uttered a sharp exclamation. What was Foster Sherwood doing with Nita at a meeting place of the Fly's men? It was strange—strange! His suspicions of the Cox heirs' guardian flashed back *again*. He shook his head. That must all come later. For the present… He moved on leaden feet toward the doctor's inner office, began to go methodically through the files. His heart was not in it, and the thought of Nita came between him and his work. An unrest fermented within him. Since this point was known to the Spider, it was of no further use to the Fly. He might well send the police here to trap the Spider. "Jackson, Ram Singh. Lookout, rear and front. Whistle if you sight police!" Jackson moved sluggishly through the office, opened the rear door, then crashed it shut!

"They're already here, sir," he whispered.

Wentworth's hand flashed to the lamp on the desk and extinguished it. He was instantly out of his seat, but it wasn't necessary to order Ram Singh to lock the front door. He had already done it. Their position was totally untenable. This was a first floor office, the windows were only about six feet from the ground and there were too many openings to guard. Besides, the Spider did not fight the police…. His usually swift brain was clogged with bewilderment. Nita must have done this. Not so soon could she have communicated with the Fly and received his orders. But why, why… He laughed sharply, harshly….

A fist hammered hard on the door, shook it in its frame. "Open in the name of the law, Spider!" a man growled. "If we have to come after you, we'll come shooting."

"You'll have to," Wentworth called back suavely. "Just a

minute before you begin hostilities!" As he talked, his hands were swiftly at work. He stripped off his wig and thrust it into his pocket, left his bushy eyebrows. He mashed the beaked nose of the Spider in a pugilist's flattened feature. "There's an innocent man in here!" Wentworth continued. "He was a patient of the doctor and got caught in the fight. Before you begin your attack, you ought to let him out. He might get hurt."

"For God's sake," cried the man in frightened tones. "Let me out. The Spider… God, I'll be killed." He ran to the door and beat on it with frenzied hands. "Let me out…."

"Wait a minute," Wentworth said, drawing the screaming man back from the door. "We'll put him out the window, then you can't use him to get in. Is that all right, gentlemen? Surely, you wouldn't want to hurt him?"

"Oh, don't hurt me," the man whimpered.

OUTSIDE THE door, voices rumbled. Wentworth turned to Ram Singh and spoke swiftly in the Sikh's native Punjabi, keeping his tones low. "Tell Jackson what I say afterward. I am

Nita Van Sloan

going to knock out this man and go out the window in his place. You will lower me.

Once I am behind the policemen, I'll create a diversion so that you can escape. Understood?"

Ram Singh's smile was in his voice. *"Han, sahib!"*

"How about it?" Wentworth shouted impatiently to the

policemen in his own voice. "I won't surrender. You should know that by now."

"All right," growled a policeman, "lower the other guy out the window, but we'll pump you full of lead if anybody tries funny stuff."

"I don't even feel humorous," Wentworth agreed. His spirits had risen with the peril. Danger was to him the stimulant that most men find in drink. It put an edge to his wits, limbered his tongue, gave him a new courage.

"Oh thank you," cried the patient. "Thank you...."

Wentworth's fingers thrust sharply against his throat, hit important nerve centers which rendered him instantly unconscious. He smiled gently down at the man as he lowered him to the floor. He would be quite safe here and he would be well repaid for his inconvenience.

Wentworth slipped two hundred-dollar bills into his limp palm, then he snatched a sheet from the doctor's examining table, tied it under his own arms and signaled to Ram Singh who was rapidly whispering the plan to Jackson. Jackson's wide, muscular jaws creased in a grin.

"I'll put him out the front window," Wentworth called to the police. He changed his voice to the whimpering of the patient. "Oh, thank you, gentlemen. This is kind of you, Spider. I won't forget it...."

Jackson took Wentworth's coat and hat, draped them over his shoulders which he hunched as best he could in an imitation of the Spider's twisted form.

"Don't show yourself recklessly," Wentworth urged. "They're likely to shoot, in spite of the truce."

Jackson nodded and Wentworth, whimpering pleas and thanksgiving was lowered out the window. The instant his feet hit the ground, a sub-machine gun stammered and—the window fell in fragments. Inside the office, there was a hoarse cry, but Wentworth could not tell whether one of his men was hit, or whether they were shamming to gain time…. Enacting his role to its utmost, he cowered to the ground for a moment, then when a policeman yelled to him he scuttled across the pavement at a swift run.

"Watch that man," a sharp voice ordered. "It would be just like the Spider to let himself out the window, and…." The voice choked off. Wentworth had reached the man, and his fingers had struck the throat nerves again. He whipped out both of his automatics, leaped to the driving seat of a parked squad car and kicked it into motion. He emptied an automatic straight up into the air. Behind him, pandemonium broke out. The machine gunner turned toward him and lead hammered over the body of the squad car. Revolvers blazed from roofs, from doorways….

Wentworth crouched to the floor. He had the squad car rolling and accurate steering was much less important than cover. For two blocks, he steered erratically, then he reared high enough to see a corner which he whirled on two wheels. Immediately he had turned out of sight of the police, he stopped the squad car and ran to the shadows, ran back toward the house where Ram Singh and Jackson were trapped!

The, police were too well disciplined, he knew, to abandon

the siege because one man had made an escape. They would bear down harder than ever, but their strength would be weakened. Some undoubtedly were pursuing, and he would have liked to lead them further astray, but it made return too slow and difficult. They would scarcely expect him to come back to the scene of the fight, though they might send some man to check on that possibility.... Over a fence, Wentworth swarmed, a—bare second ahead of the first pursuing car that rounded the corner. The radio roadster—tried to check its speed, but was skittering at the moment brakes were clapped on. It collided violently with the rear of the squad car. Before the men could disentangle themselves, Wentworth had taken a second fence....

The single cross-street he had passed was only dimly lighted, but Wentworth saw policemen at fixed posts at each end of the block. He was certain to be seen if he made an open crossing and the only alternative was to sneak up on one of them and knock him out. That would take too much time. Wentworth stepped out on the pavement and walked openly, with ringing heels, toward the street where machine guns hammered and the siege of the doctor's office was in full swing. The two policemen whipped about, guns gleaming in their hands, but as Wentworth continued openly to approach one of them, they made no move. They were waiting, suspicious, but partly calmed by the directness of the Spider's behavior....

Fortunately, one of them was on the side of the street to which Wentworth wished to cross and he angled toward the man—and toward a fence which divided a backyard from the walk. If he made a single slip—if he gave any slightest intention of his purpose before he vaulted that fence—lead would whistle at him from two directions. At any event, the moment he made his leap, the alarm would be given. Police would know that he had doubled on his trail to release his men. His actions must be lightning-swift.

Wentworth did not make the mistake of sliding toward the fence. He walked along the curbing, sizing up the barrier he must overlap from the corners of his eyes. The policeman ahead of him was off-guard, but he still held the revolver in his hand. It would be a close thing there. What the officer behind him was doing, Wentworth could only guess. To turn his head would betray him…. He picked the point at which he would take the fence, but kept his body relaxed and easy. Abruptly, he took a long, leaping stride, bounced into the air and grasped the top of the fence with both hands. Wentworth was an experienced athlete. Tumbling and acrobatics had been part of his training and he kept his muscles alive and ready by constant practice. His sudden bound sent him upward, his arms stiffened and served as a pivot and he swung his legs sideways horizontally over the fence.

He had his hands on the top of the boards before the police-man realized what was happening. The man's gun flew up then, but instead of taking careful aim, he banged away wildly. That defeated him. Had he delayed for a heart-beat to take even fleeting aim…. The lead whimpered past inches high and Went-worth dropped out of sight behind the boards.

Wentworth guessed what the policeman had done, but he had not glanced at the man once he had gone into action. Nothing he could do, once the leap was started, could avert a true-sped bullet and he must depend on his speed and the unexpectedness of the thing he did. So his eyes, as he vaulted the fence, were on the ground toward which he plunged and, seeing that was clear, he shot his gaze ahead to the space between him and the next fence. Thirty feet. Wentworth landed on his feet, but made no effort to check his momentum. He used it to somersault and came up springing. One stride, two, and he sprang for the second fence. Not until he topped that one would he be even temporarily safe from lead. If one of the policemen was an athlete and could take the fence....

There was no more shooting behind him and Wentworth took two more fences in the same swift manner and was in the yard through which the doctor's office had its exit. Men would be in hiding here, he knew, but there could be no stalking now that the enemy had sighted him. It would take time for the two policemen who had seen him to carry word to the man in charge of the raid. They were piping already, but it would take words to explain. Before that time....

WENTWORTH TOOK the last fence as he had the other two and, sailing through the air, hands still on the top of the boards, he caught the white gleam as a man turned up a startled face where he crouched behind a large dog-house. A quick glance about the yard showed one other man, nearer the building than the dog-house, but he had not yet detected this new source of danger.

The man who had spotted Wentworth's approach whipped about his gun, his mouth opened in a cry of warning. That cry had just started, the gun only half-lifted to shoot, when Wentworth hit on his feet a bare half-dozen feet away. With the impetus of his vault behind him, Wentworth arched through the air in a head-first dive. The policeman was starting to his feet and Wentworth took him, shoulder to stomach, drove him backward against the dog-house and spilled him unconscious to the ground.

It had all happened too quickly for the policeman's companion over there to know what had occurred. He caught the half cry, the sound of a fall and jerked to his feet.

"Bill?" he cried. "What the hell…?"

Wentworth crouched behind the dog-house, groping for the man's hat and his own. "Damn it," he muttered hoarsely. "I twisted my ankle…." He found the unconscious man's hat, slipped it on his head and showed himself just above the dog-house. "More damned stones…." He had one from the gravelly earth in his hand and his arm shot forward like the beam of a catapult. The second officer grunted as the rock took him in the stomach and before he could recover from the surprise and shock of the blow, Wentworth had stepped in with two swift blows that began at his toes and exploded against the man's jaw.

Wentworth stood silent for a half minute, breathing lightly through his nostrils. His blood raced thrillingly through his veins. This was the sort of thing for which alone he lived now… He puckered his lips and whistled softly, on a piercing, minor note, then he ran lightly forward to the door.

"Ram Singh! Jackson!" he called softly. "The way is clear here!"

The night echoed with the shrillness of police whistles and

hoarse shouting. The rasp of men's running feet sounded on pavement Wentworth rapped urgently on the door. "Jackson! Ram Singh!" Damn it, they would have to hurry. He had opened a way, but it would close again within brief seconds. The door jerked open under his hand and Jackson came striding out. His face was set in harsh lines and he carried a gun in one fist. Over his shoulders was drooped the unconscious form of Ram Singh.

"Got him through the chest, sir," he said harshly. "Damn them! I'd like to cut loose on them…."

Wentworth's mouth shut rigidly, but he said nothing, led the way swiftly through the yard toward the alleyway. There were sure to be more guards there. He could hear footsteps racing toward the spot. Luckily the alley ran only half way through the block, did not connect with the street where Wentworth had dodged the two cops….

His thoughts were lightning flashes in his brain. He crowded down the pain and regret of Ram Singh's fall, a glittering point of anger. Nita, Nita has caused this…. All his plans for escape must be changed. He pulled open the gate, stuck out his head with the uniform cap he had snatched….

"Hey," he yelled hoarsely. "They got Bill. Come on, and we'll rush them."

There were two men in the alley and they came, head down, guns fists pumping. Both of them were cursing in their anger. Apparently, Bill was well liked. Wentworth shouted again. "Hurry!"

HE DUCKED back inside, peered through the shadows toward Jackson. He had leaned Ram Singh against the fence and he had his right arm lifted. Wentworth nodded. They had worked together too long to have to explain a piece of action as simple as this…. The men lunged through, one on the other's heels and the two fell in a crumpled heap to the double blows. "Across the alley," Wentworth snapped. "Through the house. I'll get the car, pick you up on the next street."

"Right, Major," Jackson whispered. He shouldered his burden. When he reached the opposite fence, Wentworth was already at the street junction with the alley. He darted out, head down, zigzagging. If only those men in the car didn't have a machine gun. Thank God. Only revolvers spoke. He made them a bad target, but the fence ahead would be difficult. He would have to straighten and, for men whose guns were ready, his soaring vault would be slow and evenly timed—an excellent target. He'd have to chance it. He loosened his topcoat, let it flap behind him to confuse his body line, pulled his head well down. He checked at the curb, then lunged. He strained his muscles until they creaked to gain a tenth of a second of speed. Lead chunked into the fence by his hand. His coat jerked across his shoulders. His left arm crumpled to the hammer of a bullet.

It dropped him awkwardly into the yard beyond the fence. His leg struck the boards and sent an agony of pain throbbing up his thigh, but he was up and running instantly. His lips were motionless and cold against his teeth. He felt his left arm as he sprang for the next fence, grated his molars at the pain of fingers on the open wound. Through the muscles of the forearm, but the bone seemed undamaged, thank God! He forced the arm to operate on the next fence, and pain jabbed into his pectoral muscles. Behind him, there was an exultant yelping. They knew they had scored a hit, probably expected to find him flopping helplessly on the earth back there....

He couldn't keep on taking fences with that wounded arm. The pain of it would weaken him even if he could drive his damaged muscles to the task. He swerved sharply toward the houses on his left, ducked for the basement door, thrust his elbow through the glass.

From the darkness of the corridor that stretched ahead, a revolver blasted and Wentworth flinched backward, sped toward the next fence. His breath was whistling between clenched teeth. There was desperation in his heart. It came to him like a blow to the stomach that Nita was behind all this, had sent the police to trap him. Good God, Nita!

He drove his flagging body over another fence and the revolver cracked behind him again. He felt a blow on his right side and fell heavily on his face to the ground. He was up as if he had bounced and once more ran for a house. Oh, God, that last wound couldn't be serious. It must not be, or he and Ram Singh and Jackson.... But they did not matter. It was the fact that the Fly would triumph. Who was there who could meet his evil genius if the Spider were slain? Slain? Hell, he was as foolish as a woman. He wasn't dead yet. He elbowed out another door and, with a sob of breath caught in his throat, leaned forward into the darkness. If there was a man here with a gun.... No one shot at him and he raced along the basement corridor, found a door that stuck, and then rasped, as he yanked it open, couldn't find the catch on an iron grating that closed the area under high steps where the door opened. He found that, too, after moments of groping with almost unfeeling fingers. He heard the door in the next house burst open, heard a man's hysterical yelping....

"I shot him! I shot him! I shot the Spider!"

RAGE WAS brassy now in Wentworth's throat. Damn it, he gave his life to the service of these people and they bayed him like hounds at the kill. He slipped from the areaway, kept close to the fence as he stole along the street. If only there were no police within sound of the man's voice.

He was still screeching, but abruptly the sound became muffled and Wentworth realized the man had darted back indoors. Wentworth swerved out from the fence, lifted his knees high in a sprint. In the next cross-street, he had parked the Daimler. If only the police had not yet found it there....

Wentworth's head felt light and the pain surged through his arm. His side burned. He hoped that was a good sign, that the lead had only skimmed his side, perhaps glanced off a rib. The revolver had been of low caliber. The blast of it had told him that.... Another fifty yards and he would round the corner. He could better ten seconds on a hundred yards—but not in this clothing, of course. He counted feverishly as he strode, strode, strode. That damned revolver banged behind him again, once, twice... and he was around the corner. The Daimler! There it was. Another fifty yards. Oh, God, let—the police not be on guard there! Let them not be... Wentworth's arm crossing his heaving chest, dragged out an automatic. If the police were there.... A bullet through the leg, perhaps. Surely, to save his life, and that of Ram Singh and Jackson, to preserve the Spider for more battlings with the Fly....

The Daimler was unguarded. Wentworth flung into the driver's seat, had it rolling in seconds before the man with the revolver rounded the corner. Wentworth slowed, cranked down his window and stuck out his head. The uniform cap had stayed with him.... "Where'd he go?" he demanded excitedly. "Where'd the Spider go?"

The man waved excited arms in the air, bony wrists thrusting far out of the sleeves of his dressing gown. "I shot him, and he kept on running!" he cried. "He came around this corner. Maybe he jumped the fence. He can go over a fence like a bird. He spreads his cape and flies like a bird. But I shot him, I tell you."

"Good," Wentworth shouted. "Hold him here while I get help." He sent the Daimler roaring for the corner, took it on two wheels. His lips were twisted against his teeth. His chest still heaved. He had at least planted a false lead there if the police came. They wouldn't get much sense out of the thin man in the dressing gown.

Around the corner ahead—whirled a police coupé, siren ripping out. Wentworth ducked from its path, slapping on brakes. For an instant the coupé slowed, then, seeing that he had stopped, the police raced on. They didn't figure that the Spider would stop at the mere sounding of a siren. Wentworth sent the Daimler rolling slowly on, pulled up at the curb before dark houses. Instantly, from the shadows, Jackson sprang forward with Ram Singh still across his shoulders. He staggered a little, made the back seat and Wentworth floor-boarded the throttle.

Attention made no difference to him now. The Daimler was bullet-proof. Even its tires could scarcely be affected by lead. And if they could catch him, then the Spider had lost all his skill.

Jackson slid back the glass slide between the front and rear. "Ram Singh got it in the lung, Major," he said heavily. "Got him on the side so he won't strangle."

"Think you can fix him up at home, Jackson?"

"Oh, sure," Jackson agreed. "You can't kill anybody as tough as Ram Singh by putting a thirty-two caliber hole in his lung. Sure, I can pull him through. But won't you be needing me?"

"Always need you," Wentworth admitted, "but this time we can't stop to get the doctor. I'm going to pay a call on Lou Cox's guardian. Something is brewing in the Fly's particular line tonight. I know that. Both—the girl and her brother are in it to some degree. His presence at the doctor's office is extremely suspicious. Yes, I'll have a chat with Foster Sherwood...."

"Say, Major, begging your pardon, but I know what's up tonight." Jackson's voice was as swift as a bullet. "Phone rang while we were fighting. Thought you might be calling. Answered. Gary Cox, I think. Wanted to know why other fellows hadn't come along. Said he would be damned if he could rob the Haldorf single-handed."

"The Haldorf!" It was an oath as Wentworth—said it. The richest, most lavish hotel in the—city, where thousands—tens of thousands—of dollars poured into the coffers nightly. And the Fly, with his murderous escape methods, was striking there!

Wentworth laughed and the sound was edged with hysteria. Wounded, Ram Singh out of the fight, Nita helping the enemy, and the—Fly pressed on to his greatest villainy! Wentworth lifted his face to the damp spring sky. By God, the Fly should not win! There was still life in the Spider…!

CHAPTER 9
GREEN GLOBES OF DEATH!

WENTWORTH SHUT his mind to fury and despair, began to map his plans. He would have to warn the police, of course. The wholesale attacks by the Fly were not to be met single-handed, even by the Spider. He himself must get there as quickly as possible. He threw swift words over his shoulder.…

"Come up front, Jackson," he called. Jackson must drive Ram Singh to the apartment, then follow him to the Haldorf when he had taken care of Ram Singh's wounds.

"Just for luck, bring me whatever prints Jenkyns has developed and one from the *moulage* in the safe," he ordered. He would depend on Jackson to phone the warning to Kirkpatrick.…

A half-dozen blocks farther on, the Daimler drew to a halt beside a taxi and Wentworth flung out.

"Hurry, Jackson," he called, but his voice was drowned in the mounting roar of the engine as the Daimler spurted away. He sprang to the taxi. "The Haldorf! There's a twenty in it for you if you make it in ten minutes!"

As well as he could he dressed the wound and remedied the damage done to his facial make-up. He had the hat and cape of the Spider, taken from the supply in his car, but he did not don them just yet. The Fly must not know that the Spider was on the scene until....

The taxi rocketed around a corner, scooted in ahead of a long limousine and whirled into the tunnel entrance of the Haldorf. The driver stood on his brakes, batted up the meter flag and twisted about.

"How'm I doin', buddy?" he demanded.

Wentworth smiled as he handed the man his fare and promised reward. "I hope that I do as well," he said quietly. The driver's grin left his face.

The taxi man was not the only one to mark Wentworth's entrance. In the shadows, a man in a bellboy's uniform slipped swiftly toward a door and, once inside, he almost ran. The Spider saw him and his eyes narrowed a trifle. He doubted that he had been recognized unless the Fly was forewarned that he might come and had set a watcher. That was possible, of course. Wentworth knew that his senses should have their usual brilliant keenness for the struggle ahead, but the zest was gone out of him. He was an actor who had gone once too often on the boards in the same role. His heart was not in it—yet he would still give a creditable performance....

Where would the Fly strike first? He could loot the manager's office, where most of the money would be concentrated, without any great flourish, but that was not the custom of the Fly. He would prefer something more spectacular. Wentworth suspected that he would prefer something in which he could slaughter people wholesale. There was a perverted cruelty in the

101

man, Wentworth was sure. Why else would he delight in such massacres as he achieved? Of course, he invariably used courage to cover his escapes:

Wentworth glanced quietly about the well-known lobby, his eyes questing over the pillars of variegated marble, the balcony

The magician scaled the green globes at Wentworth!

with its rich hangings of tapestries and velvets. Nothing had been spared of luxury in the building of the Haldorf, nothing of beauty. The bellboy who had sped at sight of Wentworth entered an elevator and Wentworth watched the cage indicator as it swiveled over a semicircle of figures. Nineteenth floor. Good God, *the roof garden!*

THE SIGNIFICANCE of the bellboy's flight gripped Wentworth with painful dread. At this hour of the night the roof garden would be thronged with the most brilliant assemblage of guests in the city.

Yes, yes, that was where the Fly would choose to strike. There was less money there than in the manager's office, but nothing would prevent his sweeping clean every till in the entire hotel. He would undoubtedly choose the fabulous, glassed-in roof garden for his first blow. What form would his murder take tonight?

Even while these thoughts coursed through Wentworth's mind he was moving swiftly across the lobby toward another elevator. His eyes, which appeared never to be raised from the floor, took in everything about him.

Strolling carelessly across the lobby came Nita van Sloan, her laughing eyes turned upward to the face of her escort: Claiborne Lee! Wentworth could not fight down a stab of swift jealousy, but he mocked himself with a bitter twist of his lips. This thing was of his own doing.

He fought down the emotion, surveyed the situation as he stood aside to let them enter the elevator ahead of him. His eyes went involuntarily to Nita's face and read in its stiffened features that she had recognized him.

He kept his eyes covertly upon her as he went with an appearance of great humbleness into the car with them.... He saw Nita's lovely eyes sweep him once, saw Claiborne Lee glance carelessly in his direction. There was no recognition in Lee's gaze. Wentworth had uncovered the long-haired wig that was part of the Spider's disguise. It gave him the aspect of a middle-aged musician of the old school. If he had had a violin case in his left hand instead of the heavy cane which it cost him so much effort merely to hold because of his wound....

A suspicion Wentworth could no longer resist entered his mind about Lee. He told himself that it was born of the sudden jealousy which racked him, but the idea would not be downed. After all, Lee was going to the scene of tonight's raid by the Fly, and he was with a woman—Wentworth winced at the thought—a woman who had helped two of the Fly's men to escape from a trap the Spider had set, who had been with Foster Sherwood, who must certainly be classed as a suspect.

Wentworth studied the man as the cage moved swiftly upward. He had the build of the Fly, but that in itself meant nothing. Any man a little above average height, with good shoulders and a lithe carriage would resemble the Fly. The details of face and hair, even the color of the eyes, meant nothing. A man clever in disguise could change them all.

NO DECISION was possible at this time, of course, but when the Fly struck on the roof garden.... Wentworth considered that it would have been possible for Claiborne Lee, supposing him to be the Fly, to wear that black monk's robe in which he had appeared at the masquerade, over the costume in which Wentworth had found him. Lee also had known that Wentworth was going to interview the girl, Lou Cox, and could have followed and shot her. There was the fact that he had appeared so opportunely at Nita's kidnaping. Might the Fly not have planned that with the intention of becoming friendly with Wentworth, through Nita, and learning his plans so as to thwart them? If only he had a palm-print of this man, such as he had obtained from Charles Holland, he might verify that once and for all....

At the entrance to the roof garden, Wentworth was turned back. The headwaiter was very courteous. "I'm sorry, sir, but our rules require evening dress...."

Wentworth smiled in an embarrassed way, spoke with a thick Teutonic accent. "Ach, so," he agreed. "It iss that I wish to speak mit der *meister*, Rigau. He a countryman of mine iss. His vader mine *Freund*...." He smiled kindly, blinking the eyes that could be so bitter and cold. The headwaiter was disconcerted. Even in this mild role the Spider's personality impressed itself. The man hesitated.

"Your name, sir?" he murmured.

Wentworth whispered a famous name.

The headwaiter's hands flew high. He bowed, led Wentworth along the side aisles of the roof garden. Curious eyes turned to this blinking twisted old man before whom the headwaiter bowed so humbly. He did not even have on evening dress.... Wentworth's eyes shot keenly about him under the mask of his diffident smile. A magician, in the middle of the dance floor, was doing fantastic things with green glass globes. He was juggling the fragile spheres with breathtaking deftness. It was a master performance. Wentworth saw that the man's eyes returned to him again and again as he kept up a running fire of talk in connection with his juggling.... It was perhaps foolish, but at sight of the man, the Spider's feeling of danger mounted swiftly. Though what harm the magician could do with his delicate glass balls was hard to imagine. The spotlight which was focused on the man winked once and Wentworth saw his body stiffen with tension. He whirled clean about, his eyes flew to Wentworth and he snatched one of the arcing spheres from the air and scaled it directly at Wentworth's face!

There was no reasoning in the thing Wentworth did, but the Spider rarely had time to reason out his actions. His muscles obeyed the swift orders of his subconscious and this told him that any untoward action in this atmosphere of tension was to be viewed with suspicion. Wentworth flung himself backward, twisted and landed on his knees behind a temporarily vacant table. The headwaiter took a half-step after him and the sailing green globe caught him in the face. There was a puff of flame, a low, muffled report and the waiter screamed and reeled backward, clutching at his throat. His eyes stared blindly from their sockets, his face was mottled with scarlet splotches and about his head there swirled a small cloud of greenish gas!

EVEN AS Wentworth glimpsed these things from the tail of his eye, the headwaiter stiffened and pitched heavily forward to the floor. His face bounced and the greenish gas settled heavily downward…. Before the man had fairly fallen, the magician had hurled a half dozen more balls. They flew with a swift accuracy toward the table where Wentworth now crouched. The cloth caught fire from a puff of flame. A woman behind him screamed and beat at her shoulder which fire had dotted with crimson, then the cloud of gas found her face and she tried to flee… and fell dying.

Men and women were whipping to their feet in panic. Their shouts and screams made a cacophony of terror.

Wentworth pulled out an automatic and shot the glass sphere in the magician's left hand. The man's scream rose high and terrible. The burst of flame, the detonation, was dazzling and it flung the magician a dozen feet across the dance floor. He landed sliding on his chest, leaped to his feet and tried to flee. Flame was billowing from a dozen patches of his clothing and each one foamed with the greenish gas…. His agony was quickly ended.

Wentworth whirled about and every light in the room blinked out. From everywhere came those dull, awful explosions as from somewhere—everywhere—hidden men hurled bombs of the deadly gas. The Spider knew that he must change his position swiftly. Undoubtedly many men had been assigned the task of killing him. He darted to the dance floor and the spot he had quitted burst into flame as several of the deadly bombs burst there….

Rage twisted Wentworth's heart. What could he do against this inhuman attack? If the men had been using guns, he could have spotted them by their flashes and shot them down, but these bombs might be tossed from anywhere. The entire crowd was fleeing in wild panic from the roof garden. He could hear the brittle crash as some frenzied guests burst through the glass walls, dwindling screams as they plunged nineteen stories to their death. One thing Wentworth could do. He made all possible speed toward the manager's office where the money was kept. He could not stem the tide of panic. Indeed, flight was the safest thing for these trapped mortals. But he could strike at the leaders of this massacre and make sure that they perpetrated no more horrors....

Men and women bumped against him. A hand closed on his wounded arm and caused him torture before he could rip free and charge on to his task. He knew his way perfectly in the dark. In the pleasanter days and nights when the duties of the Spider did not harass him, he had frequented this spot of superlative entertainment with Nita at his side. In the midst of furious action, that memory could still bring him pain.

He whipped about the screen that shielded the door of the manager's office, swung into the room and his gun flew up. On the point of firing, he hesitated, a cry rising in his throat. The manager was dead, shot through the forehead. And over him, gun and flashlight in hand, stood... *Charles Holland!*

CHAPTER 10
IN THE POWER OF THE FLY!

WENTWORTH RIDICULED himself for his previous skepticism about Holland's guilt, for his failure to kill the man when his sword point was at his breast. Holland had whirled at the cry and his gun swept out, but even as he leveled the weapon, the beam of his flash brushed over Wentworth. Holland shouted.

"Wait, Spider. Wait!" He opened his fingers and his gun thudded to the floor. Wentworth's hand had already squeezed on the butt of his automatic and he could not avoid shooting. He did manage to jerk the muzzle aside so that the bullet hissed by within inches of Holland's head.

"Pick up your gun," Wentworth ordered harshly. "I do not make a rule of shooting unarmed men, but if you do not...."

"For heaven's sake, Spider!" Holland pleaded. He took a hesitant step forward, his empty hand reaching out. "I didn't do this. I came here to guard Planter. He's a friend of mine. When I got here, he was... like that."

"The money is gone?" Wentworth demanded. "Yes, Spider. See, the safe...."

The safe door hung open and papers from its interior were scattered over the thick carpeting. Wentworth hissed an oath. "I'll call on you for explanations later," he asserted and sprang out of the office again. He was not convinced, but he felt a strange reluctance to kill Holland. In those few swift minutes of sword play, he had conceived an admiration for the man's courage, for his sense of fair play. Holland had not been compelled to fight with swords. He might simply have ambushed Wentworth with the man called Shock.... Still Wentworth berated himself as he sped in the wake of the fleeing crowd. God knew the evidence against Holland was not conclusive, though Wentworth had slain men on less. It was a matter of conscientious conviction that a man was guilty which governed the Spider in his swift forays for justice. In this case, despite repeated evidence, he could not convince himself....

At the elevator doors, Wentworth halted. All of them stood open, but empty space yawned there. He peered down the shaft, throwing the feeble beam of his pocket light into the darkness. What he saw sent him reeling back, feeling nausea strike his stomach viciously. Those shafts were choked with the broken bodies of men and women!

Wentworth leaned his shoulders against the wall, sucking in deep, noisy breaths. God knew he had seen death in many forms, but this slaughter was so cruel, so utterly wanton! They had been fleeing in panic, offering no obstacle at all to the Fly's escape with his loot, and he had deliberately tricked them into a death which they thought was the avenue to escape. Heavily, Wentworth moved from door to door, closing them on the carnage below lest someone later take that fatal plunge. He whirled about, seeking Holland. If he could have seen him then, he would have killed. But the man had taken advantage of his momentary mercy to flee. That in itself was suspicious….

Hell, he was wasting time. Even if Holland were the Fly and lay dead there on the floor of the office, his men would carry on with their mad massacre. Wentworth whirled to the steps, went down them with bounding, though silent, leaps. The Fly had triumphed terribly on these upper floors, but he would not stop there. It would be in the main lobby, off which the manager's office opened that the big looting—and probably the big slaughter!—would be consummated.

A FLIGHT above the mezzanine balcony, Wentworth checked his mad race. For a breath, he paused there, listening. The sounds that met his ears were fearful in the message they carried. Lips shrinking from his teeth in fury, Wentworth hurled himself down that last flight. Gun poised in hand, he looked out upon a scene of horror which dimmed into insignificance even the massacre of the elevator shaft!

The floor of the lobby was strewn with the bodies of men and women in gala evening attire. Sprinkled among them were dead police, in uniforms and in plain clothes, fallen across weapons that Wentworth saw had exploded crazily in their hands. A few of them still were alive, huddled against the main doors of the lobby. Their faces were twisted with fear and rage. And over the whole scene crept and crawled in rolling waves... *the green gas of the Fly!*

There on the farthest edge of the tidal wave, a woman crawled with sagging head, clutching her throat with one hand while she struggled. A policeman stepped gallantly forward to help her, and pitched down beside her, writhing. The puff of flame that marked the bursting of a bomb set fire to his blue coat, but he was already dead with the strangling gas, as was the woman. One of the man's companions jerked up a riot gun in fury and leveled it at the balcony at a spot opposite from Wentworth. One of his comrades tried to knock the gun from his hand, but he must have pulled the trigger for there was a gush of flame from its muzzle and a detonation that hurled the two struggling policemen limply back against the door. Instantly, Wentworth identified the cause. It was the gas! Tremendously inflammable, it gathered and blasted when the stab of gun flame touched it off. Wentworth whipped up his own automatic, hesitated, then thrust it back into its holster. He could see now where the green transparent globes that were gas bombs were hurled. On two sides of the balcony, men in bellhops' uniforms crouched behind the marble balustrade and hurled the death dealing missiles to the lobby below. They wore gas masks, but the green vapor did not rise even to the floor of the balcony.

Creeping cautiously closer to the railing, searching for some method of attack, Wentworth saw the broad steps which curved up to the balcony. Across it, four men in gas masks fought viciously with swords while a lone man in evening dress slashed and hacked against them.

Instantly, Wentworth recognized him. He would have known that jaunty carriage of the head, the strong shoulders even if the woman who stood back to back with him had not been Nita! It was Claiborne Lee! Nita clutched a useless automatic and a slender knife. Lee made a lunge, pierced a man through the body and was instantly back on guard position again. The rapier he wielded glinted as he swept it viciously from side to side. Quick as was his recovery, he would have died then, had not Nita used her dagger. She brushed aside a point that would have pierced Claiborne Lee's side. Even above the fury of death Wentworth could hear the man's laughter ring out.

"Well played, Nita!" he cried.

He was being crowded hard by the three remaining men. At least one of them was a superior swordsman, and he kept Lee engaged while the two others tried to work past his flanks and get him from the side…. Unwillingly, admiration arose in Wentworth's breast. The man had courage, Nita had said, and he couldn't be the Fly, fighting thus the men of the Fly. Yet jealousy stabbed Wentworth. Nita fought beside Lee as valiantly as she had beside the Spider….

113

WENTWORTH LAUGHED, the sound harsh and rasping in his throat. He took his cane in his two hands and whipped steel from the wood, balanced the blade with a whipping whirl that made the rapier hiss dreadfully.

He laughed again, flung the wooden case from him and raced around the balcony. Guns might not be able to harm these killers, but a sword could not explode in a man's hand. He rounded a column. A masked man whirled to face him, eyes goggling behind the eyelets of the mask. He jerked back his hand with a small bomb on its palm and Wentworth's body straightened in a lunge that had all his fury, all his hatred and pain of heart behind it. The sword plunged into the man's chest.

Wentworth whipped it out, threw back his head and sent the flat, mocking laughter of the Spider over the scene.

"Death!" he shouted. "Death to the murderers! The Spider comes for vengeance!"

Nita heard and looked toward where he held bloody sword high—above his head. The three men facing Claiborne Lee looked up and one of them died with Lee's point in his heart, for Lee did not glance around. With a fresh vigor, he smashed against the swords of his foes…. For the moment, all save him were held in rigid tableau, fear and hope equally striking—the enemies. Before that pause was ended, Wentworth went leaping to the attack. A second and a third of the men in gas masks died before they could recover from their terror. Down—the line there, a half dozen tried to flee, but a swordsman slew one and drove the others back to their bombs.

"He is only one man!" the leader cried, lifting his mask. "Throw your bombs. He will die!"

Anger twisted Wentworth's face. A leader perhaps…. The man was awkward and twisted, a hideously malformed hunchback! Fiercely, Wentworth whipped his wounded hand to his automatic. Death stared him in the face, whether by his weapon exploding, or under a rain of bombs. There was a chance that, before the green globes burst, other gas from below would not have risen high enough to cause an explosion.

Each twitch of the trigger was agony, but Wentworth joyed in the pain. He fired, and the gun did not explode. The leader ducked into a doorway and a man leaped to guard him. Bullets hammered against the wall. His sword fell, ringing, from his hand, and he tried to brace himself. Two others of the men had fallen before his resistance died, as his body had before, and he slid sideways along the wall, rolled and hit on his face. Wentworth was emptying his gun in a swift drum-roll of death. Not one of the six who attempted to flee survived. One of them sprang over the balustrade to the deadly gas of the lobby….

Wentworth stowed away his automatic, held his sword under his arm while he drew the other gun and transferred it to his left hand. Then he raced on. Bombs were being hurled at him now across the angle where the balcony curved, but they were thrown in terror by men who feared to expose themselves to the deadly accuracy of the Spider's gun. Many of them missed and dropped to the floor of the lobby; the others fell short and burst their greenish flame upon the floor. They did not kill Wentworth, but one thing they accomplished. He knew that it would be fatal to attempt to use his automatic again....

A HUGE glass window across the front of the building crashed to the floor under a hammer of machine gun bullets and the lead crept along the balcony railing where the men of the Fly crouched. Wentworth smiled grimly as he took cover behind one of the graceful marble columns that sustained the gallery. That would be Kirkpatrick's keen mind at work. Guns would not work inside? Very well, then try them outside. The rain of bullets was having its effect. Men pitched erect to fall again in death or dive over the railing to a double slaughter below. Others turned and tried to run, but there was no retreat. At one end of their passageway was the swift sword of the Spider, and at the other they met the vengeance of Claiborne Lee's rapier. It was slaughter, but Wentworth's heart sang as he worked. There was a queer acrid odor in the air that caught at his throat and made his breathing difficult, and he recalled sharply that the gas of the bombs strangled men to death. He stopped over a corpse and ripped off a mask. A bomb almost caught him on the chest as he rose again. His sword lifted swiftly and flame ran down its steel length as it bit into the bomb. A whip of the blade and the gaseous flame was in the face of him who had hurled it....

That was the end of the Fly's attack, but no more than a score of his men had died and fully three times that many victims lay scattered on the floor of the lobby and there were those pitiful dead in the elevator shafts and on the floor of the roof garden. Money? From where Wentworth stood, he could see the open door of the manager's office and through it the looted safe.

Certainly the Fly had flown and taken with him the entire wealth of the hotel's many money sources. The Fly had flown… Holland? Wentworth frowned as he turned his back on the scene of victory and fled swiftly up the stairs he had descended. There was small hope that he would find Holland still delaying in the hotel, but if he were… Even now Wentworth was doubtful whether he would slay the man. Nevertheless, he pushed stubbornly on, found as he expected, that the top floor was empty of living men….

Well, the Spider's job was done here. He had helped to inflict a telling blow upon the Fly, though the man had succeeded in escaping with the loot. Wentworth had a plan. He hoped that Gary Cox had not been slain in the night's foray, doubted somehow that he had. It was more than likely that after his expected allies failed to arrive, due to the Spider's blow at the doctor's office, he had left the vicinity. That suited Wentworth excellently…. He rapidly took off cape and hat, stripped the disguise of the Spider from his face. His sleeve, he found, was bloody, but there would be no way for police to tell that he had not suffered the wound during the battle at the hotel.

Gripping his wrist, then, Wentworth descended through deserted halls to the main floor. The dead were everywhere and there were signs of brutal looting upon the bodies of the women. The men of the Fly, then, had not contented themselves with the money in the safes…. On the floor above the mezzanine, Wentworth opened the elevator door with a lockpick, one of the tools he always carried in a kit strapped about his waist, and, mouth grimly set, climbed down among the bodies of the dead. Some here—some few—were only injured. One woman seemed unhurt, but she held her face in her hands and sobbed softly. She did not see Wentworth as he threw himself down, in simulation of unconsciousness, among the dead....

IT WAS a half hour before the gas cleared from the lobby and the elevator door was opened. Wentworth was hauled out of the shaft with the rest. He stirred himself then, staggered to his feet. He saw Commissioner Kirkpatrick grasping the hand of Claiborne Lee, congratulating him. Kirkpatrick looked queerly at Nita, then strode off toward his men. He saw Wentworth, sprang to his side....

"You're wounded!" he cried. "By God, Dick, this is a fearful thing...."

Wentworth cursed harshly. "I was caught in the stampede. God knows how I survived that fall. I suppose bodies cushioned...." A shudder shook him. "I'm not squeamish, Kirk, but this slaughter is incredible. There must be fully five hundred dead."

A familiar figure came striding across the lobby, Jackson, with his broad, good-humored face, tortured by fear. When he saw Wentworth, his lips parted in a grin.

"Thank God you escaped, sir," he said.

Wentworth smiled slightly. "Yes, Jackson. I'm glad, too. Did you get those articles from Jenkyns?"

Jackson nodded. "You want them, sir?"

At Wentworth's assent, he reached into his pocket and took out two sheets of paper, on each of which appeared the print of a man's palm. Wentworth glanced at them and his lips closed harshly. He looked into Kirkpatrick's eyes, held out the papers....

"On the night the masquerade party was raided, Kirk," he said, "I went in the masquerade of the Spider."

Kirkpatrick interrupted, his voice grave. "That was very dangerous, Dick. Some one might have seen you and not suspected that it was merely a masquerade."

In spite of the gravity of their surroundings, of the discovery he had just made, Wentworth smiled. "Yes, some one might have. In fact, the Fly did."

The fact that Wentworth was the Spider was an open secret with the Commissioner of Police. Not that Wentworth had ever admitted it, or that the Commissioner's knowledge was generally known. But Kirkpatrick was not remiss in his duty. He had never got the conclusive proof that Wentworth was the Spider. If ever he did, he would prosecute to the full power of his office. Wentworth knew that, nor would he have it otherwise. He could respect such devotion to duty, even if it meant his own life....

"That's unimportant," Wentworth hurried on, told Kirkpatrick about the shot at Lou Cox and his finding of the palm print in the mud. "Now, compare these, Kirk," he said, offering the two sheets again.

Kirkpatrick studied them attentively. "By God, Dick, they're the same! You're saying that this is the palm print of the Fly?"

Wentworth shrugged slowly. He was frowning at the prints. "It's hard to say. You can read the circumstances as well as I. Of course, it wouldn't stand in a court of law. There is no proof save

119

my word that the original print came from a moulage made from a mud print in Holland's garden."

"It's good enough for me," Kirkpatrick said harshly. "Whose palm print is it?"

Wentworth bit his lip. Ridiculous of him to hold back now when it seemed so sure that the evidence was sound. Kirkpatrick repeated his demand before Wentworth made up his mind. He made a broad gesture with both hands, palms upward.

"Charles Holland," he said, "but I'll have to admit there's nothing surprising about his palm print being in his own garden, even supposing it was at the exact spot that the assassin was hidden. You could find out whether he works in his garden himself…."

KIRKPATRICK UTTERED a sharp exclamation of impatience. "You let him go, Wentworth," he said sternly. "I left him in your hands and you let him go scot-free."

Wentworth nodded slowly. "He was upstairs in the roof garden tonight. I saw him, with a gun in his hand, and could have killed him, but didn't. I wasn't sure, you see, Kirk. He swore to me he would surrender at any time you asked, and, damn it, Kirk, I believe him!"

"You don't believe your own evidence, Dick?" Kirkpatrick was angry. "Damn it, he's the logical suspect. It was his brother who became the Fly at first. What more natural or logical than that his brother should follow in his footsteps?"

"That's just it," Wentworth said slowly, "it's too damned logical."

Kirkpatrick's lips were grim beneath the pointed black

mustache. "Somehow, Dick, that doesn't convince me." He whirled, shouted to a policeman. "I want Charles Holland picked up at once and taken to headquarters! The charge is suspicion of murder!"

Wentworth shrugged. "I think you'll be sorry about that, Kirk," he said somberly. "There are some other possibilities as suspects. Foster Sherwood, and—" His lips tightened—"Claiborne Lee."

Kirkpatrick eyed him steadily, as he outlined the case against Sherwood. "I'll admit," Wentworth concluded, "that none of this is as conclusive as the evidence against Holland. Lee, for instance, killed several of the Fly's men tonight, but I might point out to you that the Fly cares nothing for human life and provided his men did not know his true identity, which is very likely, Claiborne Lee could provide himself an excellent alibi by himself killing his own men—if he were the Fly. Furthermore, there is always the interesting possibility, that this Fly is the Fly we thought dead...."

Kirkpatrick smiled slightly, shaking his head at that last. "I notice that you and Nita are at outs, Dick," he said quietly, "and that she is here with Lee tonight. I might tell you, Dick, that Claiborne Lee is a very clever detective of a special sort. He takes only cases which interest him and he has never, as the Spider does, gone outside the law. He is, I believe, independently wealthy... Recently, he devoted some thousands of dollars to helping the Mayor with that graft inquiry. You recall? They were very close together...."

Wentworth said drily, "Thanks. It's not jealousy that prompts my suspicions, I assure you. I concede that there is but a slight case against him. I'm merely trying to prevent serious trouble resulting from your arresting Holland." He smiled, bowed stiffly. "I think I'll be going now."

He turned away with a gesture to Jackson to follow and strode across the lobby with its crumpled dead. Nita and Claiborne Lee were leaving by the main door and Wentworth stood back to wait until they had gone. Even so, he passed them on the pavement and he was aware of Nita's eyes on his back as he moved away. They hurt, those eyes. Heaven help him, he loved her so! This damnable misunderstanding! He stumbled as he walked, his eyes blurred, and Jackson's steady hand caught his elbow. He shook his head angrily. Damn it, he was acting like a school boy! And he couldn't help it!

HE CLIMBED blindly into the back of the Daimler. Jackson sprang to the box, sat stiffly waiting for orders. Deliberately, Wentworth dug his fingers into his wound. The pain hit like a hammer. He half-swooned against the cushions, but when it was gone, all emotion had drained from him. He could think clearly again....

"The home of Foster Sherwood," he told Jackson, and the Daimler rolled swiftly forward, turned up Park Avenue and began to race the traffic lights. Wentworth sat very straight in the rear of the car. Somehow, the physical and mental pain had left his brain very lucid. He saw the way to find the Fly.... He picked up the speaking tube.

"Jackson," he said clearly. "I want you to kidnap Gary Cox,

hold him prisoner somewhere until two o'clock tomorrow afternoon. Then turn him loose within the city limits."

"Do I follow him, Major?" Jackson asked quickly.

Wentworth smiled into the darkness. "No, that won't be at all necessary. When you have released him, you will go directly to the home of Foster Sherwood and stand guard over him."

"Is Foster Sherwood… the Fly, Major? Why don't we just kill him tonight?"

Wentworth was still smiling. "The time is not ripe, Jackson. Keep very good guard, both over young Cox and over Sherwood."

He leaned back against the cushions and closed his eyes. His head still felt—light and his brain lucid, but his body was very tired. Well, after tomorrow night, he could rest…. The hard, sharp squeal of brakes jerked Wentworth's eyes wide. His hand whipped to the gun beneath his left arm, but before he could fire it, the door of the tonneau was wrenched open and a bareheaded man in a monk's robe thrust a revolver muzzle against his side.

"Don't move, Wentworth," the man cautioned pleasantly. "I would like to chat with you awhile before I kill you."

It was the Fly…!

CHAPTER 11
APPOINTMENT WITH DEATH

WENTWORTH LOOKED with a curious detachment up into the face of his enemy while the Fly flung orders at Jackson, telling him that if he did not obey, Wentworth would die. There was a small coupé just ahead of the Daimler. It had pinned Jackson to the curb and, as they passed it, Wentworth could see that it was empty. He smiled into the Fly's face....

"Very clumsy of you, Holland," he said mildly. "You don't know anything about a gun. In fact...."

Wentworth's right arm lifted in a movement too fast for eye to follow. His left hand closed over the revolver and twisted. A whimper of pain came from the Fly. He collapsed on the seat beside Wentworth, leaving the revolver in his enemy's hand. It had been a simple trick, one a man experienced in gun work never would have permitted. The muzzle had been placed against Wentworth's side—*above his forearm.* A mere lifting of the arm dislodged it. With his left hand, he had clamped the chamber of the revolver immovably, which prevented the weapon from being fired, then he had twisted the gun about so that the trigger finger was caught between the leverage of the trigger and the guard. If he had wished, he could have broken that finger....

"Stop the car, Jackson," Wentworth called softly. "Now, Holland, get out. I'd advise you to strip off that disguise as quickly as possible. It's pretty good for an amateur, and it just possibly might convince the police that you're guilty. By the way, Kirkpatrick has ordered you picked up. I'll remind you of your promise to surrender when I gave the word."

Holland's shoulders were slumped far forward. "Why didn't you kill me?" he whispered miserably. "You could have so easily."

Wentworth laughed. "So you saw Gary Cox at the Haldorf!"

Holland stiffened, whirled about. "You know! For God's sake, Wentworth, spare the kid. He doesn't know any better. He's smart, but he has moral sense. All these killings mean nothing at all to him except…. Don't kill him, Wentworth."

The Daimler had stopped. Wentworth handed his revolver back to Holland. "Get out and surrender yourself to Kirkpatrick," he ordered. Holland started to plead again, looked into Wentworth's eyes and marveled at the thing he saw there. Tenderness and sympathy in the eyes of the Spider! Holland got out and stood staring after the Daimler as it rolled down the Avenue. He looked down at the revolver in his hand, laughed at it and flung it across the street. He turned and strode toward the car he had been driving….

In the Daimler, Jackson said, "Good God, Major. You let him go. You must be awful sure…." Wentworth spoke wearily. "We must kill the Fly, but Charles Holland is not the Fly. We must kill also the man who invented and makes that death gas. If I live through tomorrow, we will win, but within an hour the Fly will know that the game is up. It will be very strange if he lets me live… after that."

THE SHERWOOD mansion was set well back from the street, an ancient brick building almost castle-like in structure. It was one of the first of the large Victorian houses, of atrocious architecture, but containing scores of rooms. Wentworth knew its history intimately, as he made it his business to know all such matters as might some day be—needed by the Spider.

It was—supposed once upon a time to have been used as a base for smugglers who brought goods up across the wide

The bullet smashed the machine gunner's head, hurling him back!

127

lawn from Long Island Sound. The huge gate that formerly had swung between the stone posts of the entrance had long since been unhung and the Daimler purred throatily as it swept up the gentle rise to the house.

Wentworth walked with deliberate dignity up to steps from the *porte-cochère*—he had disguised himself a little—and the door opened without a signal. The butler who stepped back deferentially was a man of studied inconspicuousness. He gained that effect partly by keeping his eyes continually lowered, partly by an eager clinging to the shadows. However, there was a strength in his face that belied the meekness of his manner. Wentworth noted these things without seeming to as he fingered a card from his case.

"Mr. Sherwood," he said.

The butler showed him into a reception room, turned his back to leave the room and Wentworth sprang like an arrow from the bowstring. The blackjack he had palmed thudded gently upon the base of the man's skull and he caught the butler as he collapsed. Instantly, he had his back to the wall, eyes sweeping the walls, the windows and draperies of the room. If he was right in his suppositions, death might strike at him without warning any minute during his stay in this house. His mere presence here would warn the Fly that his secret was at least guessed….

The dark silence of the house brooded and Wentworth edged to the door, peered along the dim hall.

Gas was still used for illumination and a red-globed lamp near the ceiling threw a pale, lurid light. Wentworth skirted its pool and went soundlessly up the steps toward the second floor. For all his caution, he moved with surprising speed. The blackjack still dangled from his wrist. He did not draw a gun.

On the second floor, he paused for a moment, listening, then he went directly to a door that showed a thread of light. No sound there, except the occasional rustle of paper. He crouched to the keyhole, could just see the foot of the bed, whose head was against the wall of the hall. There was a negligee of pale blue draped over it. Wentworth straightened, tapped gently on the door with his knuckles. At the girl's gay "Come in?" he thrust open and, in a single bound was beside the bed with his hand over Lou Cox's mouth.

Her eyes flew wide in tortured fright. Her body wrenched violently. Wentworth smiled gently. "Please," he whispered low. "I want to talk with you, and I was afraid you'd give the alarm. Will you promise to remain quiet for a few minutes?"

LOU'S EYES rolled upward and her weight slumped against his hands. Wentworth released her and instantly she screamed, piercingly, on a terrified note. Wentworth laughed. It had been a neat trick. His finger tips prodded the side of her throat and the girl slumped unconscious on the pillow. It was a painless method.... Swiftly, he hurried into the hall. He could hear swift, heavy footsteps below.

"Lou!" a man's voice called anxiously. "What is it, Lou?"

Wentworth made his voice deep and somber in imitation of the butler who had received him. "Begging your pardon, sir, Miss Lou saw the curtain move and it startled her. She says she's sorry, sir."

The man at the foot of the steps hesitated, peering at the

shadowy upper hall. His face was heavy beyond his years, his hand upon the banister below was lean and strong. It was Foster Sherwood.

"Ask Miss Lou if she wishes me to come up," he said finally.

Wentworth responded, "Yes, sir." He moved soundlessly away from the head of the steps, opened the door of the girl's room, after a knock, closed it again. Then he returned to the shadows at the head of the stairs.

"She says no thank you, sir. She's sorry for the disturbance."

Foster Sherwood shook his head, turned and moved heavily away down the hall. He walked as though a great weight rested upon his shoulders. Wentworth's eyes were hard and speculative…. When the footsteps had died away, he went quietly to the girl's room. Before he wrapped her in bedding and carried her soundlessly to the car, he thrust the knife he had taken from the Fly's victim and dug its point into the door….

Jackson set the Daimler into instant motion, and Wentworth smiled at the startled stiff line of his back. Obviously, Jackson had not expected a kidnaping….

"It is necessary, Jackson," Wentworth said kindly, "to save her life."

Jackson said, "Yes, Major." Some of the stiffness went out of his poise. "Where to, Major?"

"Home," Wentworth said quietly. He was busy with a small hypodermic set he had taken from the compartment behind the left-hand seat. He mixed morphine and, after listening to the girl's heart, nodded his head and made an injection in her left arm….

They carried the girl in through the service entrance. The superintendent of Wentworth's building knew better than to inquire into anything that transpired on that elevator....

IT WAS noon the next day that Wentworth arose from a deeply refreshing sleep. He showered, submitted himself to a rub-down at the expert hands of Jenkyns, then went to inspect his prisoner. Lou Cox still slept deeply. He listened to her heart again, counted her pulse and breathing, nodded in satisfaction. She would begin to rouse from the drug shortly and within an hour should be fully recovered. Jenkyns would have his story prepared for her. Wentworth had surprised her kidnapers, brought her here because he was ignorant of her identity. Naturally, she was free to leave at any time.... It was one o'clock. In an hour, Jackson would release Gary Cox, her brother, from captivity. The newspapers already had headlined the story of Lou's kidnaping by the Fly....

WENTWORTH'S LIPS were smiling grimly as he moved toward the front door of the apartment, accepted top coat, hat, gloves and cane from Jenkyns. By tonight, the Fly would be dead, or else the Spider. He reached for the doorknob....

"Pardon me, Master Dick," Jenkyns murmured, "but will you be home for dinner, sir?"

Wentworth laughed sharply, "That's in the hands of the gods, Jenkyns."

"But, Master Dick," Jenkyns hesitated. "Miss Nita was to come here for dinner tonight, you recall, and...."

"That will do, Jenkyns!" Wentworth's voice rasped in his throat. He whipped open the door, started out, and checked, his eyes tightening. He stepped back and bowed. Nita van Sloan stood there. An eager smile had lighted her lips, but that faded now and left her mouth bitter and tight.

"I'm going to talk to you," she said quietly. "I came to warn you that the Fly knows your plans, and is expecting you. Claiborne Lee asked me to come and tell you, or…." There was a quiver of emotion in her tones. She was obviously holding herself in check with extreme difficulty. "I was well aware you wouldn't talk with me on the phone."

Wentworth had his hands behind him, clasping his stick. The knuckles were white. He bowed formally. "Very kind of Mr. Lee, I'm sure. Would it be impertinent to ask why he thinks the Fly knows? He wouldn't be the Fly himself, would he, and you his ally?"

Nita laughed shortly, and it was very like the bitterness of Wentworth's own voice. "How ridiculous, Dick. As to the warning. It is plain the Fly would have no reason for kidnaping Lou…. and I know your methods. If you refer to the little affair at Dr. Learning's office, I'll explain. Claiborne has been employed by Foster Sherwood to attempt to save his nephew, Gary, from being utterly ruined by the life of crime he seems to prefer. Naturally, that involves destroying the Fly, so I have been helping him at his work. He knew about that post at Dr. Learning's office and I went there in an attempt to worm—my way into the Fly's organization. I saw a chance—to curry favor with the Fly by helping his men, so…" Nita shrugged. "I received his thanks and a thousand dollars by mail, but he refused to use me in the future."

Wentworth would have given much to be able to drop this stiff and hostile role, as his heart cried to him to do. But he couldn't. "Allow me to congratulate you on your speed in cementing friendships," he said acidly, "and on your cleverness at Dr. Learning's office. And on sending the police so promptly. They wounded Ram Singh severely."

Nita's violet eyes had fires in their depths. Her voice was dulcet. "I learned from you, sir." She ducked him a courtesy. Wentworth had rarely seen her angry. There was a dimple there at her mouth corner—it came from the compression of her lips—that was enchanting. The music of her voice swept him as it always had, struck a vibration deep within his breast. He pulled his eyes away from her lest they betray him, then looked back lest he show his weakness. God, why must she be so lovely, so infinitely desirable. What were they quarreling about?

Wentworth was surprised at the lightness of his voice, "Thank you for your warning. I rather thought I would be expected by the Fly. If you'll pardon me now, I wouldn't like to keep the Fly waiting...."

Nita nodded her consent with perfect poise. Never had her round little head seemed so proud, nor her violet eyes so arrogant. His memory flitted back to the time they had first met, on the old Mauretania, bound back from Europe. She had been breathtakingly lovely in that cream satin gown that had set off the clear beauty of her shoulders and arms. There had been a lilt in her voice. God, the years that had passed since then....

His voice said, "Well, I must be going. May I see you to your car?"

He was still looking at her, despite that dry burning in his eyeballs. He saw her sway a little before she swept past him toward the outer door. Jenkyns' eyes were pitiful as he bowed to her, and for a moment she paused, smiling....

Wentworth said harshly, "Remember your instructions, Jenkyns!" The door closed gently behind him and they walked to the elevator.

Nita's head bowed, her hands were knotted before her. She went from the elevator without looking at him and got into her car. But when she had turned the first corner, she parked beside the curb. And she beat her small, white fists on the steering wheel; she shook her head, eyes closed, teeth set on lip. And the sobs came anyway....

She whispered, "Oh, Dick... Oh, Dick...!"

Wentworth turned blindly down Fifth Avenue. He had gone two blocks before he recalled that he wanted his roadster and that the car was parked in front of the apartment house. He went back and the doorman opened the car for him and stood watching as he sent the Hispano-Suiza sharply out into the traffic stream. A taxi stopped with screaming brakes. A Fifth Avenue bus swerved wildly. Wentworth sent the Hispano up the street at forty miles an hour.... Gradually, he calmed himself. After today, he swore, he would go away... if he survived. There was a good chance that he wouldn't, if the Fly awaited him. He smiled thinly. Well, Nita had said he would be waiting.... The street blurred before his eyes. He blinked steadily until he could see again. He was glad abruptly that the Fly knew. Death could solve so many problems....

CHAPTER 12
STOP THE GAS!

I T WAS three o'clock when Wentworth turned into the driveway to the Sherwood mansion. The place looked even drearier by day than at night. The whole, bleak pile was a dusty gray and the black shine of the windows added to a mournfulness that was singularly oppressive. Very appropriate, Wentworth jeered at himself as the Hispano whispered up the driveway.

The same dour butler who had opened the door for him the night before was waiting. If he recognized his assailant, he gave no sign. Wentworth's disguise had been the scantiest. That had been deliberate. He watched the butler narrowly, waited in the reception room while his card was carried to Foster Sherwood. Wentworth kept a keen watch about him. If the Fly was ready for his arrival.... The butler came back soundlessly, announced in his deep voice that Mr. Sherwood would see Mr. Wentworth.... The way led along the dim hall, to the door of a book-lined study. Sherwood arose from behind his desk....

"What can I do for you, Mr. Wentworth?" he asked pleasantly, but still he carried about him that sense of overpowering weight. He was haggard, his eyes sunken....

Wentworth said quietly, "I have been trying to get a line on this man who calls himself the Fly, and I thought that there might be some clue here. Do you have any idea why he should have kidnaped your ward?"

Sherwood shook his head heavily. "None at all," he said, but he did not look at Wentworth as he spoke.

"Surely, you must have some," Wentworth urged. "Or if you haven't, perhaps her brother, Gary...."

Sherwood's face seemed to become more haggard while Wentworth looked at him. He said hoarsely, "Gary has disappeared, too."

It was at that moment that the thing Wentworth had expected happened. Footsteps beat swiftly along the hall, the door flung open and Gary Cox flung himself into the room.

"Have you heard anything from Lou?" he demanded savagely.

Sherwood looked at the youth without a word, then came sharply to his feet. "Where have you been, sir?" he demanded harshly. "These disappearances of yours must stop!"

Gary sliced the air with the edge of his hand. "Nuts! How about Lou?"

Wentworth got to his feet deliberately. "I have a very poor opinion," he said sharply, "of a man who will consort with the kidnapers of his sister. Where were you when your sister was kidnaped?"

Gary whirled toward Wentworth, his right arm crooked, hand at his coat pocket. "Who the hell are you?" he demanded.

Wentworth smiled slightly, but made no other answer. Sherwood came around his desk. "Gary, this is serious," he said heavily, but even in his reprimand there seemed a lack of sincerity, of force. It was as if he were afraid of this young man before him. Gary Cox swung about to face him again.

"Where were you when she was kidnaped?" he demanded in

turn. "Here in your study, so they could get up here without…."
He choked the words and both he and Sherwood looked toward
Wentworth. Wentworth nodded his head slowly.

"That's exactly what I think," he said, "that the old smugglers'
tunnel was used to carry away your sister, Gary."
BOTH OF the men started violently and Sherwood began a
quiet movement to get closer to Wentworth. Gary Cox openly
put his hand into his coat pocket.

"The game is up, gentlemen," Wentworth said quietly. "Are
you going to lead me to the tunnel, or shall I call in the police
to find it?"

Sherwood and Gary Cox both leveled guns. Sherwood was
much the more frightened of the two. "What in God's name are
we going to do now?" he asked hoarsely.

"Conk him," said Gary savagely, "and then I'm going and…."

"Shut up!" Sherwood said roughly.

Wentworth smiled. "All right, Jackson," he said quietly, looking behind them.

The two men whirled about and Wentworth's left fist shot
out, caught Sherwood on the jaw and throat, hurled him unconscious to the floor. Gary Cox whirled, his gun blasting. Wentworth had made no attempt to block that shot. He was half
behind the desk and he went down with the flash, threshed
his legs and clapped a quick hand to his forehead, then let it
fall away. Gary Cox sprang to the end of the desk, gun ready,
saw the red smear that Wentworth had made on his forehead
and whirled away. When he darted through the door of the
study, Wentworth was already on his feet. He followed swiftly

as Gary Cox ran for a door that opened near the end of the hall. A gun stabbed flame at him from the door and he fired twice, three times in hammering succession. The butler reeled out of the doorway and plunged to his knees. He had his gun in both hands and tried to lift it upward. Gary kicked him in the throat and went past him to the door....

Wentworth waited until he had ducked through the opening, then he darted after him. He could hear Gary's feet beating hollowly on steps that led downward and moments later, Wentworth dodged through a door that gave on the cellar. He crouched and peered between the railings, saw Gary squeeze in behind a huge furnace set against the wall. He seized a metal hook that protruded from the stone, twisted it violently and pushed. The stones swung inward. Instantly, there was the muffled chatter of a rapid-fire gun. Gary was driven back against the furnace. He tried to lift his revolver and the sub-machine gun kept cracking. For moments, the bullets held him against the furnace. Then they stopped and Gary wilted to the floor.

While the gun still spoke, Wentworth had flung himself to the basement and darted across to the furnace. He waited until the sub-machine gun ceased and, a split-second afterward, he thrust arm and head around the edge of the hidden door and fired a single shot. The killer was seated behind a breast-high shield of steel on which he rested the Thompson gun. But he had counted on no second enemy. The bullet smashed through his head, hurled him backward. The Tommy gun balanced for an instant atop the shield, then crashed to the floor.

When it hit the ground, Wentworth was already inside the

opened door, automatic in one hand, cane in the other. He twitched the cane several times and let the wooden sheath slide from the steel rapier it covered while his eyes quested over the dim stretch of corridor that reached away in both directions from this spot. Electric lights burned at regular intervals, making little yellow pools in the darkness. Queer how criminals always preferred dimness to light, underground warrens to ordinary strongholds. Bad about Gary's death, but he had died more splendidly than he lived—killed on the way to defend his sister. In the moment before his death, he had triumphed over the evil influences that had held him so long. It was time for him to die. Living, he would have lapsed again into the old ways. A man who had glutted on slaughter by the side of the Fly....

An annunciator squawked abruptly from somewhere nearby: "What's keeping you, Hank? Report what happened."

WENTWORTH REACHED Hank's body in a single long leap. "Aw, I just bumped that Cox punk," he growled. "He come at me shootin'." He kept his voice low and hoarse. The annunciator would disguise it sufficiently, if there was a connection near him. It might be that he was supposed to report in person....

"Well, Hank," repeated the annunciator. "What's keeping you? Report!"

Wentworth shrugged slightly, his lips smiling calmly. He had made that play and lost. He was supposed to report in person and he had no idea how to do it. The corridor led in two directions. He would chance going to his right.

He walked with heavy, confident strides along the corridor to the right, keeping a sharp eye on the shadow patches for trace of the opening which must be somewhere near. It was plain that there was some room hollowed out of the earth. The annunciator was silent, whether because he had made the right move, or because the speaker had become suspicious, Wentworth did not know. Either way, they must make the first move, and make it soon, or else....

The collapse of the floor beneath his feet was without any warning at all. Wentworth plummeted downward with no chance to do more than cross the sword over his breast so that it would not harm him, then hit violently on his feet, allowed his knees to bend under him and sprang instantly erect. The room in which he stood was white-walled and illuminated by a single overhead light. On all sides, there were the black openings of loopholes for gun muzzles and all of them were filled. Twelve guns were centered on Wentworth's body....

"Ah, my dear Wentworth," purred a voice that Wentworth instantly recognized. "You have, I see, come into my parlor."

Wentworth tossed his automatic to the floor, took his rapier in his right hand and made it sing through the air; then he stood with the point resting on his toe. "Yes, Fly, I am ready," he said quietly.

He felt the utter hopelessness of his position. There was no need to look for mercy from the Fly, nor for compunction in such wanton murder as had been planned when this room was built. He had the slim chance of an appeal to the man's love of swords, which he well knew. Even if the Fly entered the arena, there would be no fair fight. Wentworth was doomed....

There remained, though, the chance that he might kill the Fly before he was slain. That was Wentworth's only hope. To death, he was indifferent. Tonight, he might even welcome it. A weak thought, unworthy of the Spider. Was he a woman to pine away over a lost love? So Wentworth mocked himself while he waited, superbly ignoring the hungry gun muzzles. It made no difference. He knew that, without Nita, life held nothing desirable for him, and though he reviled the selfishness of that realization, it did not alter the fact.

"Afraid of my sting, Fly?" he called gaily, shaking the rapier over his head. "Afraid of your skill?"

The Fly spoke slowly, meditatively. "It would be madness for me to duel with you, but it is madness toward which I am inclined. I have never crossed blades with you and you defeated Holland. Yes, I am inclined to meet you. Holland was an able man...."

WENTWORTH HEARD other voices in colloquy with the Fly, but presently a door opened and the Fly stepped into the white-walled room. Wentworth saw that the man had expected the duel, for he wore the knee-trouser, the white blouse of the fencer and his feet were clad in light-weight, rubber-soled shoes. Wentworth stuck the point of his rapier in the floor and stripped off coat and vest. The Fly stood watching, a mocking smile on his lips.

"Are you quite ready?" he asked when Wentworth grasped his rapier and tugged its point free of the floor. "Quite," Wentworth agreed.

The Fly lifted his blade to a guard position and as simply as that began the most perilous duel Wentworth had ever known. Over him hovered in striking down the Fly, he would not survive him by so much as one minute! Those ominous gun muzzles assured him of that…. Both men fenced cautiously in those first interchanges, doing no more than feint for openings. The blades slithered in almost constant engage and there was no sound in the close room except the music of the steel and the low, constant shuffle of cautious feet.

Wentworth instantly discovered that the Fly had a powerful wrist, that his finger play was facile and accurate. They were both hesitant about making the first lunge. Wentworth saw an opening, but instead of striking into it, leaped backward a full three feet. It was the instinct of a swordsman that impelled that and he could tell by the chagrin that darkened the Fly's face that he had acted wisely. Even now, Wentworth could not decipher what trap he had avoided and the fact made him doubly cautious.

Usually impetuous in attack, Wentworth decided to out-wait the Fly, to make him reveal his reach and speed. The Fly did not falter when the opportunity was offered. With the speed of a cobra, he hurled himself forward in a lunge, body in a straight line behind the rapier. It was a beautiful attack, perfectly executed, but Wentworth's parry was irreproachable, and his answering lunge was fiery and vicious. The Fly was back in position and avoided the licking tongue of steel doubly by guard and backward.

Both men had tested the mettle of the other, but Wentworth was not satisfied with what his enemy had revealed. That lunge had been swift, but it had lacked the drive of a master swordsman and there could be no doubt that the Fly was that. It seemed clear to him that the Fly was playing a waiting game, too, attempting to lull him into security by slowing his lunge. When he really struck, with his full speed, his point would be in before the timed parry so much as touched his blade. It was fine strategy and might have succeeded on a man less experienced than Wentworth. He knew, however, that no man with that splendid recovery should be so laggard in attack.

Lunge and parry, thrust and *riposte* made a regular rhythm and Wentworth realized that in spite of himself he was slowing his guard to the speed the Fly set. It was necessary, of course, to do that, but he must not allow his reflexes to become laggard. There was a cure for that…. Wentworth began an attack so fiery, so furious that before it the Fly gave cautious ground. He lost his smile for moments, then Wentworth played the trick for which he had planned. He pretended to let his attack grow uncertain and ill-directed, made his breath come in labored pantings. He blundered wide in answering a feint and leaped back as if in desperation as the Fly's point licked out in the flicker of an eye. THE SPIDER avoided it with seeming clumsiness, but the rapier did not get through and the swift attack that the Fly immediately began failed to find the slightest opening. Fury darkened the Fly's face as he realized that he had been tricked into displaying his real speed. He continued the attack, thrusting, lunging, inching forward to pin Wentworth against the wall. Once, twice, three times Wentworth barely avoided the point. His shirt front was ripped; there was a scratch on his throat and another on his forearm. Nor had the Fly escaped unscathed. Wentworth had scored low on his side and the point had penetrated half an inch before the Fly's backward leap had cleared him. His shirt was stuck to his body with a sprawling red stain....

The increasing delay shortened the Fly's temper. It was clear to Wentworth that no man had ever stood thus before the sword of his enemy. Impatience made him reckless. He gave opening after opening and Wentworth, pretending caution, broke away. He did not cease to counter, for that might arouse suspicion. But his retreat was none the less steady. His back was within only six feet of a corner, now only five as he skittered backward. The Fly began a vicious attack. If he could squeeze his enemy into that corner.... Wentworth intended him to do precisely that!

Minute after slow minute dragged past as Wentworth fought with seeming desperation against the trap into which he was being driven. Finally, he sprang back from a long, fierce lunge and his shoulders hit the wall. It was the moment for which Fly and Spider had both played. The Fly closed in, poised himself and lunged again! If his point broke through Wentworth's guard, there could be no further retreat. He would be pinned to the wall!

Wentworth turned the point with his sword, seized the Fly's blade with his left hand and yanked him strongly forward. At the same time, Wentworth sprang toward the Fly, dropping his own sword backward through his hand until he gripped the blade only nine inches from its point. The Fly gasped, tried to spring backward, but Wentworth's grip on his enemy's blade had become a grip on his wrist; then about his waist. With his arm locked about the Fly, he sprang backward into the corner and pressed his sword point against his enemy's side.

"Quiet!" Wentworth gasped, "or I'll kill you!"

Shoulders against the wall, the Fly held motionless against his chest under the threat of that sword point against his side, Wentworth was completely shielded from all the gun ports!

"Now then, Fly," Wentworth said, more quietly. "You can order your men away from those gun ports or die!"

The Fly was stubborn and before Wentworth could convince him that refusal meant death, the door opened again in the side of the room and a half-dozen swordsmen in gas masks stalked through. At the same instant, Wentworth was aware of the trap door being opened overhead. A bone-thin arm reached through, holding a huge chemical retort, from whose beak greenish vapors rose. The liquid in the retort began to stream toward the floor. It struck and greenish flames danced upward, greenish fumes roiled toward Wentworth and his prisoner!

The Fly cringed against Wentworth. "The death gas!" he gasped. "Oh, God, *stop the death gas!*"

CHAPTER 13
NITA UNDERSTANDS

THE TERROR of the Fly seemed entirely genuine. He struggled in a veritable frenzy of fear against the grip of the Spider. Yet it seemed strange to Wentworth that an underling of the Fly would deliberately release the death gas upon his master. The Fly wore no mask, had no chance of obtaining one while he struggled, breast to breast, with the Spider.

Wentworth's position was sufficiently perilous without the additional hazard of the gas. He was locked in a death embrace with the greatest terror of modern crime. The thought brought a laugh to his lips, strangely exultant laughter. He set his left hand against the chest of the Fly and hurled him back upon his fellows. He whipped up his rapier and struck swiftly. One of the masked men died. Even as he fell, Wentworth was upon him, ripping off the gas mask. Then he fell back into his corner, back to the wall, rapier weaving a swift tapestry of light and death before him.

It was awkward work, getting the mask on one-handed. For a space of seconds he would be blinded. Wentworth shouted his challenge. There were five swords against him, and one of those was the Fly, one of the most superb men with the rapier that Wentworth had ever fought. Yet, before the whirling impetuosity of Wentworth's attack, those five men retreated. Wentworth sprang far back, thrust sword-tip into the floor and, working with both hands, whipped the gas mask into place. Instantly, he had the rapier in hand again. He even had time to glance upward toward where those emaciated arms, those claw-like hands poured the green liquid of death down upon them. He could see now a face twisted horribly by hatred, a hunched back and a great cry rose in Wentworth's throat. He knew that man! Good God, it was…!

Wentworth's thoughts were chopped off short by a whirling attack in concert by the swordsmen. Three could face him at once across his narrow corner, and the Fly took the brunt of the attack while the two men, one on each side, crouched low and stabbed at Wentworth with their long blades. Still the swift, wild sweeping of Wentworth's sword kept their points from a vital spot. A rapier stung him in the thigh, and the man who wielded it died a moment later with the kiss of Wentworth's steel upon his throat. He was immediately hauled away and another man took his place.

The mask-covered faces were strangely blank and featureless, not even the eyes could show expression through the thick lenses of the goggles. Wentworth's own mask made his breathing difficult. The nose clamp had his nostrils raw. He—attempted a foray from his corner, but a rapier darting at his heart flung him back. He managed to parry that thrust of the Fly. Another blade stabbed up at him from the floor, ripped through his coat.

Wentworth swept the swords wide with a beat of the rapier and, from behind the three men who faced him, a fourth hurled his rapier like a spear! Wentworth snatched it from the air, spun it in his hand and was doubly armed. Laughter bubbled unbidden to his panting lips, came muffled and hideous out through the mask. The man at the trapdoor had ceased to pour out the deadly liquid. He held a revolver in his hand now and it was leveled at the Spider's head. His time had come—but he preferred steel to that bullet from above. Steel and a chance to kill….

HE FLUNG himself forward with such fury that his assailants retreated—two of them. The third took the point of Wentworth's second rapier in his breast. There was no time to

147

withdraw it. The man writhed on his back and the rapier, upright in his breast, swayed like a flower in the wind. Three men left to fight. Strange that they did not use their guns, for Wentworth was sure now that the gas was a fake. A thought struck him sharply. Perhaps this gas contained only the elements which caused guns to explode in the hands of the firer. That would explain the reluctance of the Fly's men to use their automatics....

Wentworth had only one defense against that revolver above, the speed of constant movement. Not for a moment could he remain still for the murderer in the trapdoor.... The constant exertion was telling upon the Spider, further handicapped by the mask. Despair ate at his heart. He was fighting not alone for himself. His own life was a small part of what must drive him on. Unless he killed the Fly and that other twisted monstrosity there in the trapdoor, the slaughter of the people would continue. Thousands of lives fought with him, the ghosts of slain hundreds powered his blade.

Abruptly, the Spider saw his chance. With a violence and a speed that literally defied vision, he hurled his body forward in a long, low lunge that brushed aside the Fly's parry as if it were no more than a silken strand and sent the point deep into the Fly's chest!

Instantly, Wentworth released his hold on the hilt and hurled himself aside. He was too late. The sword of the Fly's henchman licked out and caught him on the right side. It was no more than a shove against his flesh, but Wentworth knew from the instantaneous weakness that gripped him that it had bitten deep. His body was already in motion and it helped some, dragged him away from the sword. Wentworth's hand seemed leaden as it moved to his automatic. At least he could get one shot with it. The weapon would explode, but certainly that one bullet would fly true. He heard the crash of a shot, felt no blow. That monstrosity above had missed once, at least.... The gun was in Wentworth's hand. The swordsman had pulled his blade clear and was poised over the Spider for a last murderous lunge. It did not matter to him that the Spider was helpless, flat on his back. Now, at last, the Spider would die!

Wentworth ignored that swooping sword. He still must kill that fiend who had invented the green poison, who leaned through the trapdoor, gun in hand.... It was to him that the Spider's eyes went. For a space of what seemed seconds, he could not understand what he saw there, but actually his vision darting to that grim creature in the trap door, and the movement of his gun must have been simultaneous. He saw that the scrawny hand in the trapdoor no longer held either gas retort or revolver. The body sagged limply forward and from the side of the head, there came the slow drip of a dying man's blood. The Spider's one shot then, need not go to save humanity. It could save—his own life, perhaps.... He squeezed the trigger of the automatic and heavy caliber lead hammered into the chest of the man with the poised sword. It lifted him inches from the floor and spun him away—and the gun did not explode!

WENTWORTH LAUGHED out crazily against his mask. He pushed himself up from the floor, pressing his hand hard against his side where the sword had pierced. The blood was warm on his palm. Awkwardly, Wentworth thrust the automatic into his belt, tugged at the mask. His first guess had been right. The gas was a fake, used to disconcert him in an effort to save the Fly. He got the mask free, gripped his automatic again. The man he had shot lay on his face, not even twitching. He looked upward, toward the—trapdoor and a glad cry parted his lips.

"Nita, sweetheart," he panted. "Nita!"

He reeled forward, reaching up as she swung down a light rope ladder she had dropped through the opening. He lost his footing, and on his knees crawled on until he could reach the ladder. Nita dropped on her knees beside him, began ripping at the clothing about the wound. Her face was white, lips between her teeth.

Wentworth was strangely numb to pain. His eyes joyed in Nita's alarmed face. "You should… smile," he whispered. "This is the end of all your troubles. You won't be kidnaped… any more."

"Keep quiet, Dick," Nita said. "Save your strength, until I see…." She tore aside his shirt and a cry rose to her lips. She bent close, fingers moving with gentle firmness along the rip in his side. Then she leaned back, tears rolling down her dimpled cheeks. "Oh, Dick, Dick," she cried. "You gave me such a scare. I think he splintered the bone of one of your ribs a little, but it's not deep." She bent close. "Dick, boy, don't ever say cruel things to me again. I thought I knew why you did it from the first. You wanted me to spy on Claiborne Lee. But afterward… I didn't know."

Wentworth closed his eyes. They were stinging and it wasn't from the fake gas that had been poured into the room.

"Promise me, Dick," said Nita, her voice very close to his face. "Promise me you'll never be cruel like that again."

Wentworth laughed. "You think it has been pleasant!" he cried. "Damn it, Nita, you played your part too well. Even I thought you had thrown in with the Fly! And there was the time you sent police helter-skelter to Leaming's office...."

Nita held up her hands. "But, Dick, you always get out of those jams so easily! I thought it would be no trouble to you—the back door and all. I didn't think you'd even be there, and it made my position so much stronger!"

Wentworth's eyes burned up at hers. "Yes, I see now. I should have seen then. There's a madness that gets in me when the Spider walks.... And then I found out I had thrown you to the Fly.

"Claiborne Lee," Wentworth told her briefly. "He's over there, dead with my rapier in his breast. He is the Fly. You'll find that's the truth when the disguise is stripped from him."

"But he couldn't be!" Nita cried. "He *couldn't* be. I saw him kill..." She hesitated. "Of course, that would give him a perfect alibi, killing the men of the Fly, and he did know a lot about the Fly. How in the world, Dick, did you come to think of that, and of this place under the house, these tunnels...?"

"It was ridiculously simple," Wentworth said quietly. "I should have known it long ago. The clue was the murder of the Mayor. God, how long ago that was! There was absolutely no reason for the murder of the Mayor that I could discover," Wentworth said slowly. "I hadn't thought much about it until I learned that Claiborne Lee and the Mayor had been very close together.

None of the other suspects had any contact with him at all, and there must be some reason other than mere spectacular crime for the murder. It reduced itself to the fact that the Mayor was killed because he knew… who the Fly was! It would have to be that, or revenge. And so far as I have been able to discover, the Mayor lived a pretty blameless sort of life… These tunnels here? That was more obscure. Except that I couldn't see any reason for Gary Cox being an important member of the Fly's band. He was a youngster without any of the training for criminality, without any reason for going into it unless he was deliberately lured into it. That was one of the things that cleared Holland in my eyes. I couldn't see how, loving Lou Cox as he undoubtedly did, he could seduce her brother into a criminal life. Then it became clear to me that Foster Sherwood was somehow involved. I remembered the history of the house, the reports of secret tunnels. So I kidnaped Lou and her brother Gary, finally turned loose Gary after the fact that the Fly was supposed to have kidnaped his sister had been revealed. I followed him to the Fly's hideout… and the rest you know."

"Most of it," Nita admitted. "Jackson was watching over Foster Sherwood when I came here. I tried to get him to investigate the shooting I heard down here when I came here to… to meet Claiborne Lee. He wanted me to see you killed!"

Wentworth smiled. "You couldn't blame him. I think he really loved you."

Nita shuddered. "God grant that he didn't," she whispered.

Wentworth looked up into the dead face of the monster who had poured the gas. His eyes were filled with wonder. "The Fly really did come to life, Nita," he said, "and he poured out his hate against me and against the world."

"You mean… Jack Holland?"

Wentworth nodded. "Yes, it's plain that he was crippled terribly by that fall after our duel. If you will look up there in the trapdoor, you will see him."

Nita looked up at the man who had poured the gas into the room, who had so narrowly missed killing Wentworth.

"That man!" she cried. "Why, I…!"

"Yes, dear," said Wentworth softly. "You killed the real Fly."

www.ingramcontent.com/pod-product-compliance
Lightning Source LLC
Chambersburg PA
CBHW052139170626
46812CB00004B/1511